CRAZY FOR THE BOSS

CRAZY IN LOVE #1

ASHLEE MALLORY

Copyright © 2016 by Ashlee Mallory

2nd Edition Copyright © 2017 by Ashlee Mallory

ISBN: 978-0-9970035-6-7 (E-Book)

ISBN: 978-0-9970035-4-3 (Paperback)

Cover design: Letitia at RBA Designs

Copy/Line Editor: Amy Knupp at Blue Otter Editing

1

Two dollars and thirty-five cents. Two dollars and forty-five—

Ooh. A quarter... Getting closer.

If only Quinn's place in the line leading to the coffee cart was getting closer. Two customers closer, to be precise, which would put her *in front* of the couple with no apparent boundaries to their PDA, instead of *behind* them. Thank heavens she hadn't eaten breakfast on her rush out the door this morning or she might have risked losing it all now.

Oh, man. Was that her tongue?

Pushing the image from her mind, Quinn Taylor resumed her search, digging out another handful of change and adding it to the count for the large cup of coffee she desperately needed to survive this Monday morning's settlement meeting.

"Next."

Finally. Almost there.

Seriously, you would think that this couple could get a room. From the fancy brown Italian loafers and the formfitting blue suit the guy wore, he could clearly afford it.

As if sensing her attention was on him, the guy turned his head toward her. And winked.

For the love of—

But before she could formulate a response—or pull her jaw from the ground—he returned his attention to the woman in his arms.

Quinn might have abandoned her place in line had the heady aroma of freshly ground coffee beans tangled with the salty sea breeze coming from the San Francisco Bay not wafted in her direction. No, she wouldn't give him the satisfaction of seeing her flee, especially now. She would just have to avoid eye contact until it was her turn.

A few minutes later, as she stepped up to place her order, the Adonis and his playmate were no longer in sight.

With the steaming hot coffee in hand, Quinn reached the lobby of the building for today's meeting and headed to the elevators, careful not to drip on her new white shirt. She pushed the button and waited, using the time to run through her prepared opening remarks. The last thing she wanted was to look like an amateur attorney who'd never negotiated with such high-powered attorneys and clients, even if it was true.

With four minutes left on the clock, the elevator door opened and she stepped inside, pushing the button for the twenty-seventh floor.

"Hold the elevator!"

Quinn bit her lip, looking at the time again. She could just pretend she hadn't heard them. She crept into the back corner, out of view of whoever was coming. It wasn't like she was actually pushing the close button.

The doors began to shut and Quinn relaxed her shoulders. Still with plenty of time—

A large hand shoved its way between the doors, stopping them from shutting. She closed her eyes. So close.

"Good Morning," someone said entirely too cheerfully.

Quinn opened her eyes. Of course it would be him. The guy from the coffee cart, only this time without the suctioning force of his girlfriend's lips on his face.

He stepped on, glancing at the floor number she'd already selected. "Looks like we're heading to the same place."

She forced a smile and nodded before taking a sip of the coffee, needing the reinforcement. The burning pain from the still hot brew brought tears to her eyes, and she coughed.

"You okay?" the guy asked, his blue eyes sparkling with humor.

"Perfect," she managed between her clenched teeth.

The guy didn't say anything more, but as the elevator swept upward, she was aware of his gaze on her, a smug smile playing at his lips that told her he knew exactly how perturbed she was at his presence.

The elevator opened and Quinn rushed out. Her client, Laurie Hill, was waiting outside the glass doors leading to Thornhill Management, her smile strained.

"Laurie, hi. You weren't waiting too long, I hope."

While Laurie recounted a long bus ride and getting off a stop too early, Quinn was aware of the tall Adonis continuing down the hall, walking inside the same glass entranceway where she and her client were headed.

"Quinn Taylor and Laurie Hill for a meeting with Dennis Monson," she said to the receptionist a moment later.

"Of course. They're expecting you now," said a perky brunette and escorted them back.

Immediately, the butterflies that had temporarily been grounded from this morning's frustration took flight and swirled around, beating uncomfortably in her belly.

Whatever happens, don't let them see you sweat.

Pinning her businesslike smile on, Quinn led Laurie in, noticing the full contingent already seated on one side of the oval-shaped table. She greeted Nadine Wells, the lead attorney for one of the top firms in the Bay area, along with two of her associates, followed by Dennis Monson. Dennis was general counsel at Thornhill Management who'd headed the internal investigation for the company, and who Quinn had been stuck dealing with since she helped Laurie file her complaint.

Everyone was here except for the current CEO of Thornhill Management, Cyrus Thornhill, who she'd been told wanted to be present at today's meeting. "Will Mr. Thornhill not be joining us?" she asked.

"I'm afraid that Cyrus Thornhill won't be able to make it today," Dennis said in that snide, condescending way of his. "He suffered a myocardial infarction Thursday night and is still recovering from surgery."

A heart attack? This was the first she'd heard of it. Quinn looked around the room in confusion. "Did we need to reschedule today's meeting?"

"Not necessary," Dennis continued. "The board members held an emergency meeting on Friday and have named an acting CEO who will step in while Mr. Thornhill recovers. We are waiting for him now."

This was a little frustrating. Quinn had been counting on Cyrus Thornhill's reputation for integrity and professionalism to help push them toward a fair and reasonable settlement. She knew nothing about this new guy, this wild card, and as someone who liked to know precisely what variable she was confronting in any situation, this just wouldn't do.

"I would be more than happy to reschedule this matter for another time if you and this temporary CEO..."

"James Thornhill, Mr. Thornhill's grandson," Nadine added.

"If Mr. James Thornhill would like to properly assess the situation," Quinn finished.

The door swung open and all eyes turned to the door.

Quinn's breath slowly hissed out as she saw who was standing there.

"Good morning. I'm sorry if I kept you all waiting," said the elevator guy as he stared directly at her. He didn't appear surprised to see her seated in front of him. Unlike her.

Mr. James Thornhill, she presumed.

Crap.

JAMES BIT back his smile at the look of horror on the prim brunette's face as he walked into the room. Her reaction made getting here at this ungodly hour almost worth it.

"We were just about to get started," said Dennis in a tone that told James his late entrance had been noted and marked against him. The old fart hadn't changed. "Let me introduce you to everyone."

James nodded to each person as he or she was introduced, but it was the brunette from the coffee cart whose introduction he was most interested in making, something that Dennis took his time in getting to last.

Quinn Taylor. An odd sort of name for such a serious-looking woman. And like before, when he'd caught her stern stare of disapproval at the coffee cart, she stared at him again with similar disapproval.

"It's a pleasure to meet you all." He sensed Dennis getting antsy to take the floor but James ignored him as he addressed the room. "Before we get started, I'd like to say a few words. Maybe see if we can save ourselves a lot of time this morning. I've looked over Ms. Hill's complaint and believe that we can come to an understanding short of having to file any claims or lawsuits. I'm prepared to offer Ms. Hill twenty thousand dollars to settle this right now."

Dennis coughed in fury, trying to catch his attention. Considering that Dennis had refused to make any concessions in the months leading to this moment, preferring to drain the company of potentially hundreds of thousands of dollars in legal fees to giving the woman a single dime, his reaction to James's words wasn't a surprise.

It was Quinn Taylor's reaction that he was curious about. Instead of appearing as excited at the number on the table as her client, her gaze turned more speculative. He waited while the lawyer whispered with her client another moment, then turned her sharp brown eyes to him.

"Ms. Hill would be happy to see this settled at thirty-two thousand dollars, which includes twenty-two thousand dollars for lost wages and ten thousand for emotional damages."

"Young lady, if you think that—" Dennis started to say, but James raised his hand to stop him.

"Would you like the moon, too?" he asked, raising a brow at the woman's boldness.

"Not at the moment."

And for the first time since James had met her, the

woman smiled. An actual real smile that illuminated her face, one he couldn't help but return.

With her hair pulled so tightly back, the overly large owlish glasses perched on her nose, and the frumpy skirt and jacket better suited to a nun, James had assumed Quinn was probably somewhere in her mid to late thirties.

Until she smiled.

He amended his earlier opinion. Quinn Taylor was smart, assertive, passionate...and far more attractive than he'd previously given her credit for.

"Well, Ms. Taylor, we could end this now," he drawled, taking a seat so he could meet her gaze better. "Tell you that we'll talk again after you've filed your grievance with the proper governmental channels. You'd then wait months, maybe even a year, before you were issued a right-to-sue letter. It would be at least another year before this reaches a courtroom. And in the meantime, your client will be waiting, hoping for her day in court, where she might win a landfall—or lose and come away with nothing."

Instead of looking chastised, Quinn Taylor had fire behind those brown eyes as she leaned forward. "Yes, that might be true. However, should the other Thornhill employees who have reached out to Ms. Hill decide to file similar lawsuits, I imagine it might put a serious damper on the negotiations to acquire a certain coffee franchise in the near future."

Now, how on earth did she know about that?

Of course, anyone with business ties to the West Coast had probably heard that Blossom Brew was hoping to expand its reach to the area in the next couple of years, and that they were negotiating with several companies. It had been why, on the same day the board appointed James as CEO, Thornhill Management joined the ranks of companies vying for the franchise. Thanks to a back channel James created, their chances were looking good.

At least they had been. Having a pending lawsuit that could potentially turn into a class action would seriously dampen the negotiation, something Ms. Taylor had anticipated.

He'd underestimated this woman, and instead of stoking his anger, the realization actually made him laugh. "Touché, Ms. Taylor. So let's talk about some other possible numbers."

"You're not seriously considering negotiating with these people, are you, James?" Dennis demanded.

"Let's hear a little more about what Ms. Taylor has to say."

Dennis's face flushed with emotions, his front-combed hair parting to reveal a bright red forehead. If James had his way, he'd fire the guy and his antiquated, old-school ways. But Dennis had been with Thornhill Management for thirty years and had a number of friends on the board who wouldn't take kindly to his dismissal.

Sure, James had the reins of the company, but that also meant that, at quarter's end, he'd be the one who would have to stand and take the heat for the decisions he'd made. If he screwed this up, he'd be out of here if a majority of that board thought he couldn't do it.

But as James saw it, he would go big or go home. His grandfather had built Thornhill Management—a restaurant management company with over a hundred restaurants running up and down the West Coast, from Baja to Seattle —from the ground up. Only in the past decade, as Cyrus's health suffered, so had the company in the scarcity of fresh new ideas needed to invigorate the place. Something James hoped to bring to the table with ideas like the Blossom Brews acquisition—along with a few others.

Some of the ideas coming to him the longer he sat here.

Because if he wanted to pull this company from the Middle Ages, James needed someone *he* could trust to help him make those changes. A person who might share the same values and vision he had. Someone of strong resolve who wouldn't back down from a fight. Someone who wasn't Dennis.

The idea was forming as he watched Quinn Taylor consult with her client again, her concern for the woman evident in the way she treated her with respect and kindness.

Quinn was exactly the kind of person he needed on his team.

JAMES WAITED to approach Quinn Taylor with his proposal until after Dennis and the attorneys had exited the room an hour later and she was packing up her notes, having told her client she'd talk to her once she saw the draft of the settlement agreement his attorneys were drawing up.

"Ms. Taylor. Could I have a minute of your time?"

She didn't bother to look up. "I don't think it's appropriate that we're in communication outside the presence of your attorney. If you have questions for me, you should direct those through him."

"I don't think that will be necessary. What I want to speak to you about has nothing to do with this case, rather I wanted to discuss a possible offer of employment."

That finally got her attention. "Employment?"

"Why don't you take a seat? This won't take long."

"I prefer to stand."

Of course she did. "All right. I want to offer you a job. Working here with me."

Quinn shoved the last of her things into a bag and slung it over her shoulder before heading to the door with more speed than necessary. "No thanks. I have one."

"Yes, and you appear to be doing a spectacular job." He opened the door, letting her pass before walking alongside her. "You definitely bring a sense of passion to your work, and it's exactly that passion I want to bring on board."

She reached the elevator and pushed the button. "Sorry. Like I said, I have a job, one that I enjoy immensely. I'm sure you could find someone equally competent, and without a conflict of interest as I would have."

He smiled, not about to back down. "Only, there is no conflict of interest. Not anymore. The case is settled." He studied her, trying to see if she would stay unflappable after what he said next. "I could start you off at two hundred grand a year, plus there's a nice holiday bonus, profit-sharing opportunities after your first year, and a generous healthcare package."

Her lips—fuller and poutier than he'd previously appreciated—parted, and her eyes widened. If the scuffed toes of her shoes, the cheap polyester of her blouse, or the handful of change he'd caught her counting earlier were any indication, James was certain that this sum wouldn't be something she could ignore.

The elevator opened and, instead of getting on, she paused as if she was considering his offer.

"Here. I'll see you out," he said, stepping inside as she followed.

"What kind of job are you offering exactly?" she asked.

"You would join our legal department as a special

employment counsel. As you probably noticed, Dennis is already so swamped handling things like the company's lease agreements, contracts and licenses, and landlord disputes that he doesn't have as much time as he should to stay abreast of his other responsibilities. Responsibilities like reviewing disability and pregnancy accommodation requests for our employees, sexual harassment complaints, wage and hour laws, and I'm sure a dozen other things that you could tell me about. You could be the person who employees can go to when they have questions and concerns that might be beyond the skill level of HR. Think about it. Had you been around when the events that Laurie alleged had surfaced, would you have handled things differently?"

She rolled her eyes. "What do you think?"

"Which is precisely what I'm saying," he said and grinned. "We need you here. And if you won't do it for the money, do it for all the employees whose lives you could potentially improve." It was a bit heavy-handed on the savior angle, but she seemed to be considering it.

They had reached the first floor, stepping out as the elevator doors opened. James worked to keep up with her as she raced to the exit. "Look. Why don't you take a day or two to consider my offer? Mull it over, draw up a pros and cons list, whatever you need to do." He took a card out of his breast pocket and handed it to her. "It's one of my old business cards but the phone number is still correct. You can let me know what you decide."

Reluctantly, she took it and dropped it into her bag without reading it.

"Fine. I'll let you know."

"Great. It was nice meeting you, Quinn Taylor. I look forward to hearing from you," he nearly shouted as she waved to him over her shoulder, already halfway out the door.

He'd take the fact that she hadn't thrown his card on the ground and spit on it as a small victory. For now.

Because now that he'd decided that he needed Quinn Taylor on his team, he wouldn't accept anybody else.

2

"You can't possibly be thinking about saying no to this guy," Tessa said, topping off their glasses with the rest of the Pinot Noir later that night.

Quinn had just finished telling her two roommates about the outlandish proposition that James Thornhill had dropped in her lap. She almost questioned her own sanity as to whether the whole exchange had happened or if she'd made the whole thing up, since it seemed almost too good to be true.

Two hundred grand was nothing to balk at, not when she owed half that amount in student loans, not to mention her mom's medical bills.

It wasn't like she'd be giving up some already amazing job. As a new associate at a law firm with only two other attorneys, she didn't even have the luxury of her own office space. Instead, her computer was squeezed in the back conference room, something that required she work else-where whenever it was in use. It wasn't a terrible job, since she did enjoy the work, but frills there were not.

"And the guy does make a point," Anna chimed in. "As

the head of this employment subdivision, you could make a difference to a lot of people. Did you know that Thornhill Management has more than three thousand employees?"

She nodded, having researched the company back when she initially took Laurie's case. She wasn't surprised that Anna knew this number off the top of her head either. As a writer at a local online news magazine, *The Daily Rundown*, Anna seemed to know everything about anything that might relate to the city and its inhabitants. Sure, Anna was currently stuck on the entertainment news beat at the *Rundown*, which was a nicer way of saying gossip writer, but she had aspirations to someday be paid to write feature news stories, real human-interest pieces that weren't just about some dirt she dug up on the celebrity of the day.

Anna took a drink of her wine and scrolled through the pages of stories that a quick Google search had found on the company. "This Blossom Brew thing could be a pretty big deal. It would mean opening a slew of new stores in the next couple of years."

"I love their coffee," Tessa said, returning to the couch with her glass of wine. "I hope there'll be one around here. So what about this James guy? Other than he sounds like a real hound dog, making out in the middle of the street."

"Before today, I hadn't even heard of him." Something that Quinn had immediately remedied the moment she got back to the office. "It was a lucky guess when I hinted at the whole Blossom Brew negotiation. I had heard they were talking with a couple of companies in the area and it seemed likely they would be one of them."

"Well, it worked. Here, Tessa. This is the guy," Anna said and turned the laptop so she could see the screen.

"Oh, my," Tessa said, her hazel eyes widening as she

stared at the image. Curious, Quinn leaned over to take a look.

Good Lord. Quinn snorted. Why did it even surprise her that he would be caught frolicking in the surf with not just one, not just two, but three buxom girls who, according to the caption, were all previous *Playboy* bunnies. Surprise, surprise.

"Look at those abs, though," Anna said, grinning at Quinn. "The rest of him isn't too bad to look at either."

All true. Quinn had never denied that the guy was hot. She'd just chosen to look past that.

She took inventory of his many assets. Tall, with rock-solid muscles. Dark golden-brown hair with California sun-streaked highlights. Impish blue eyes that flashed too bright with humor—usually at her expense.

Sure. He was most girls' dream. That is, if you didn't mind dating a playboy who probably dated a different girl every day of the week and who had the moral compass of a toad. A toad that likely worshiped at the altar of gold and money was her bet. Having dug the guy's business card out, Quinn had learned he used to be at a venture capital firm that, according to the website, James and a buddy had started up a few years ago and since turned into a multibillion-dollar success.

Sure, some people might give the guy kudos for making something from nothing, but in her opinion, just because he happened to know a lot of people with money, money they were willing to let James play with, didn't convince her that he'd worked any harder than she had putting herself through three years of law school. Only difference was he was now rich and she was definitely not.

Quinn took a big drink of wine, shaking her head. "I can't see myself working for the very people who I went to law school in the first place to fight against. Managers, government bureaucrats, and senior corporate officers who have no compassion for the people who work for them."

Okay, so maybe she had a bit of a grudge against those same people. But having seen what had happened to her mom—the sweetest and hardest-working person Quinn knew, who had worked over thirty years as a middle-school teacher only to be treated like she was a burden the moment she got sick—could anyone blame her? Just because her mom's illness hadn't been as tangible as something like cancer or heart disease didn't make it any less real or valid.

"Hey, do either of you want the last slice of pizza?" Tessa asked.

"All yours," Anna said, pulling her long honey-blonde hair up and wrapping an elastic band around it. "I'm going out for a run. Care to join me?"

Quinn and Tessa shared a look of horror.

Anna laughed. "Fine, but the invitation is always open," she said and headed to her room to change clothes.

As she had so many times before, Quinn thanked the skyrocket-high San Francisco housing market for forcing her to find such incredible friends and roommates. She and Anna had met as undergrads after Anna placed an ad for a roommate. Two years later, when Anna graduated with her journalism degree and Quinn started law school, they'd added Tessa—who Quinn had met her first day of torts—to their tribe.

And even though Quinn and Tessa had graduated from law school two years ago, the cost of living hadn't improved, and with student loan debt hanging over their heads, the women had decided to continue to live together. They'd pooled their limited resources from working entry-level positions in their respective fields to move to a three-bedroom, three-bathroom duplex a short walk from Alamo Square Park in the northwestern area of the city.

The place was perfect. Recently restored with higher-end appliances and upgrades, it still managed to retain its century-old identity and charm with the old wooden floors and a few distinctive architectural accents. More importantly, since they were still only a couple of years out of school, by splitting the rent three ways, they were able to stay well within their budgets.

Tessa bit into the pizza, studying Quinn. "Okay, now that you've given us all the reasons you can't work there, I think it's time for you to own up and admit how intriguing this offer actually is."

"I'll admit that the opportunity to make a difference in the lives of all those employees does have some appeal. Not the least is training some of those knuckleheads to know that it isn't going to substantially burden anyone if a pregnant woman needs to have a stool at the register," Quinn added, remembering a story one of Laurie's friends at work had shared.

She stared at the numbers she'd already played around with since she got home. Such as an estimate of how long it would take her to pay off the medical bills and her student loans with the money James was holding in front of her like a carrot. It had always been disheartening that for the past two years she'd been forking out half of her salary on those bills and didn't have anything like a nice new car to show for it.

Six months. At that proposed salary, within six months she could have the medical bills paid in full and almost twenty percent of her student loan paid off instead of the current decade she'd previously estimated. In a year, even better, that is, if she could hold out that long.

"I suppose, even if working there was as soul-sucking miserable as I would imagine, I could tough it out a year, bank the money, and get some more experience under my belt," Quinn said in a thoughtful tone. "Worst case, Fred might still have an opening in his conference room for a new associate."

"Exactly," Tessa said, Miss Glass Half-Full, her exuberance contagious. "You said yourself that you were only working for Fred for a couple years before moving on. This opportunity is almost too good to be true."

"That's what I'm afraid of." Quinn bit her lip, another possibility forming in her mind. "I suppose that, since he's wooing me to come to the company, maybe I could make a demand of my own."

"I would," Anna said, returning to the room in her running tights and racer-back bra that she pulled a sweatshirt over. "It's a process of the negotiation. Okay, I'll be back in thirty."

Quinn stared at the wall for another minute after Anna left, wondering if she was really about to do what she was thinking about doing.

"Want me to get your phone for you?" Tessa asked sweetly.

"The guy probably already forgot who I was," Quinn grumbled. But she already had made up her mind, so almost begrudgingly, she uncrossed her legs and came to her feet. "Fine. I suppose it doesn't hurt to give him a call before he forgets our entire conversation."

Taking her wine with her, Quinn headed up to her room. She shut the door and climbed onto the bed, staring at his card.

James Thornhill II. Seriously? Could he have more of a

pompous title? Heaving a sigh, she pushed the numbers in and waited.

He answered almost immediately. "James Thornhill."

She rolled her eyes. Really? Who answered like that? "Yes, Mr. Thornhill. It's Quinn Taylor. I was calling to talk to you about your job offer."

"Ah, Ms. Taylor. Glad to hear you've been giving my offer some consideration." There was definitely an edge of humor in his voice. "Did you call to see what the profit-sharing plan entailed?"

"That's not what I'm interested in hearing about right now. I actually have a counter offer for you."

"Of course you do."

She ignored that. "One thing that I noticed about your company's medical benefits in light of Laurie Hill's situation was that it was sorely lacking an EAP."

"EAP..."

"An employee-assistance plan. EAPs can provide short-term counseling service for employees who might be struggling with dependency and other mental health issues. Studies have shown that the minimal cost of adding such a plan more than pays for itself in reduced absenteeism and attrition. And had something like this been in place for Laurie who, if you read her complaint, had been suffering from PTSD after being sexually assaulted, she would have had access to the right medical provider who could have diagnosed her sooner and gotten her the counseling she needed. Not to mention she would have been educated about the process of applying for FMLA so she could have protected her job before your company fired her."

Okay, so Quinn was a little passionate on the subject. Mental health care was important to her, though, after seeing what had happened to her mom.

"Are you still there?" she finally asked when the silence stretched too long for her comfort.

"I am. But I warn you, Ms. Taylor. Any change or addition to the company's current medical benefits is going to need the approval of the board. However, I think what you're proposing sounds important and I'm one hundred percent in support of it and will do my best to champion it. You might have to help me in my presentation to the board, maybe put together some graphs and statistics to support what you're saying. Everyone loves graphs."

He was going to give it to her. Well, give it to the employees, provided they got the board's approval. She would make sure that she presented it in such a way they couldn't say no.

"Does this mean we have a deal, Ms. Taylor? You're going to join us?"

Heaven help her, she was going to do it.

"I suppose it does," she said in a voice that sounded of defeat.

"Well, cheer up. I'll be sure to have my assistant send you a state-of-the-art fruit-and-cookie basket on your first day."

"Great. I will need to give my two weeks' notice to my current employer."

"I wouldn't expect anything else. I'll have my assistant call tomorrow to schedule a time for you to come in and speak with our HR department. They'll be able to answer any questions about the profit-sharing agreement and all the rest. I'll also have Dennis get started on drafting your employment contract. After I break the news, of course."

"He doesn't know?"

"He will."

She paused, not having previously considered this

prospect. "Under this arrangement, will I be reporting to Dennis?"

This was make-or-break. She couldn't possibly work in a place where that man had any control over what she did or didn't do.

"No, you'll be reporting only to me."

A smile crept across her face at the prospect of seeing Dennis's face when he heard she was coming on board. "Okay. I guess we'll be in touch."

"We most definitely will."

ON A BRIGHT and unusually sunny day for mid-November in San Francisco, Quinn walked up to the front entrance at Thornhill Management and stared, trying to still the lingering doubts plaguing her mind that she'd made a mistake. That she'd sold out to the other side. The Dark Side.

Well, the contract had been signed and her other job was probably in the process of being filled, so she'd better just come to terms that this was where she'd thrown her lot for the next year of her life.

A few minutes later, she stepped out of the elevator and onto the twenty-ninth floor of the building. Apparently, Thornhill Management filled three of the top floors, with the executive team on the highest. After she identified herself, a tiny nymph of a woman with a pixie haircut and wide smile arrived to show her around.

"I'm Jeannie, and I help Dennis with the leases and landlord issues for our restaurants, type up contracts and memos, that sort of thing," she explained as she led Quinn down the hall. "I'll be assisting you, as well, so don't hesitate to ask me for any help."

Twenty minutes later, Quinn's brain flooded with the dozen names of people she'd been introduced to, Jeannie made the last stop of the tour: Quinn's office. "If you need me, you can press two on the phone, or my desk is just right over there."

"Great. Thanks, Jeannie."

She watched the woman walk away before turning around to check out her office. It was not only twice the size of the conference room where she'd worked before, but with the large floor-to-ceiling windows, she had a stunning view outside at the financial district. She might have gasped as she drew near.

How did anyone ever do any work with that view?

Fighting the urge to take a video of the place with her phone to send to Anna and Tessa, Quinn began unpacking the few things she'd brought for her first day from her bag. Particularly the ceramic turtle with a hidden compartment in the underbelly filled with her stash of peanut butter M&M's that she set reverently on the corner of the desk.

She was just about to steal a couple of the candies when there was a knock on her door, and she whipped around guiltily.

James Thornhill II in the flesh. Looking stylish and charming in a black tailored suit and a crisp lavender shirt that he somehow pulled off—and quite well. As he no doubt knew.

"I trust you're finding everything you need?" he asked, stepping into her office and looking around.

"So far so good. Jeannie already gave me the grand tour."

He took a seat in front of her desk, looking like he owned the place—which she supposed he kind of did. He set a set of papers in front of her and she glanced down. A contract, it looked like, for the Blossom Brew deal. "Do you think you could take a quick look at this for me? Dennis and I are scheduled to meet with a few of the Blossom people later today to discuss it."

"Um, Mr. Thornhill—"

"James. I insist."

"James," she said, not liking the familiarity of his first name on her tongue but not seeing much choice, "you do realize that my forte is more on the matter of employment contracts, EEO policies, and wage and hour reporting, not"—she looked at the papers again—"franchise agreements."

"Yes, but you've shown yourself to be nothing if not a determined person in the short time since I've known you. I'm sure if you put your mind to it, you could probably pick up a few things."

She stared at him, trying not to notice the stunning blue of his eyes or the fact that his hair had grown a little longer since she last saw him and the front of his dark golden-brown hair wanted to arch forward over his brow. Which meant he had to slide his hand up almost without thought to push it back down.

Pulling her gaze away, Quinn picked up the contract and began reading.

"Dennis already looked it over first thing this morning and seemed to be satisfied," James continued while she turned the page. "But I prefer to have a second opinion."

"Uh-huh," she said almost absently as she kept reading.

Blah, blah, blah. A few words she recognized, terms of art from her property courses.

Wait.

Something didn't seem quite right. She read it again.

She turned it around and pointed the paragraph out to James. "I don't think this clause here is correct. As it reads currently, the duration of this subsection could continue into perpetuity. It needs to be more closed-ended."

He turned around, scanning her desk for a moment before grabbing a pen. "Here, why don't you jot down your thoughts, highlight anything you have questions about, and I'll fax it over to Nadine to hear if she agrees with you. What are your plans for this afternoon?"

Her plans? Since she was still getting her bearings, she really had none yet. "What do you need?"

"Like I said, Dennis and I are meeting some Blossom Brew people today and I would like you to accompany me. Having your perspective on things would be enlightening."

"All right. Will they be coming here?"

"Actually, we're flying out to Chicago to meet them. My driver will be here at eleven to take us to the airport. Can you be ready?"

She blinked. Chicago? They were going to pick up and head out to Chicago, just like that?

"Don't worry, we'll be taking our plane so we'll have you back by dinnertime."

Our plane? As a daughter of a coal miner from a small town in northern Idaho, Quinn could count the number of times she'd flown on any airplane on one hand. It had been more economical to drive back and forth between her hometown and college over the years. And here he was actually proposing they just jet off to Chicago in their own plane?

But she could play it cool. "I guess Chicago it is."

"Great. Why don't you hold on to that," he said, nodding toward the contract still in her hand, "look it over, and then get it back to me in the next hour." He came to his feet, heading to the door, where he stopped. "Oh, by the way, I have you scheduled to meet with some of our top executives this week, and Paul Jansen will be taking you out to a few of our restaurants to get a feel for our operations. See you at eleven."

Quinn had never had the pleasure of meeting Paul Jansen before, but she had heard about him from Laurie. He'd been the upper manager who had made the final call to fire her. Quinn couldn't say she was looking forward to spending any more time with him than necessary.

She looked around her office again, noticing how much bigger it seemed now that James had left. Pulling out a legal pad and pen, she began writing a list of priorities that she wanted to focus on for the week, starting with studying up on franchise law.

Instead of feeling overwhelmed by the quickly growing list, however, Quinn had to admit to feeling a jolt of adrenaline hit her.

Jeannie knocked on her door a little later. "Mr. Thornhill thought you might want to review these before this afternoon's meeting."

"These" being a four-inch stack of documents that the woman set on the middle of the desk before heading right back out.

Quinn waited until she was sure the woman was gone before flipping over her trusty tortoise and grabbing a handful of M&M's from its secret compartment. Now all she needed was a six-pack of Coke Zero and she'd be ready to push on through.

It would be just like back in law school, cramming before an exam.

Tossing a handful into her mouth, she went off to the break room with pocket change to see what she could find.

3

"James, I really need you to review these documents and sign off on them," Quinn said, walking into his office Friday afternoon, nearly one month later.

James took a swing at an imaginary golf ball, holding his pose for a long ten seconds before glancing back at her with a grin. "How'd I do?"

Seriously? He had nothing better to do?

"Frankly, I haven't a clue. The responses are due tomorrow with the Oregon Civil Rights Division," she said, holding them toward him.

"I'm sure that whatever you prepared will work nicely."

"I'm sure, too, but like I told you, there were some red flags that came up when I was talking to a few employees about some possible management missteps. Some missteps that make me think we might want to mediate these. And, like I was saying last week, we really need to start some kind of regular legal training for our management. You wouldn't believe what one of these guys said."

He looked at his watch. "Okay. How long do you need?

Because I'm actually supposed to be somewhere. Perhaps we can go over this on the way to the airport?"

The airport was only twenty minutes away. "I'm going to need at least an hour."

"All right. Come along then. I'm heading to San Diego for a couple hours. You'll have my undivided attention almost the entire trip. No distractions."

She hesitated. "We'd have to be back by seven."

"Hot date?" he asked, resuming his imaginary golf game. His jacket off, sleeves rolled up past the forearm, and the top two buttons of his light blue shirt undone, it was hard for Quinn not to stare at the picture he presented with his shirt hugging and displaying every muscle of his arms and chest, the breadth of his shoulders, not to mention the tight, firm roundness of his—

She shook her head in disgust. What was she doing?

"It's my roommate's birthday and we're taking her out to celebrate."

"Then let's be off."

Nearly two hours later, the car that had picked them up from the private airstrip pulled in front of a Mexican restaurant. There was a line of people hovering by the entrance that was decorated with bright Christmas lights shaped like chili peppers.

That's right. Christmas was only a week away.

"James? Why are we stopping here?" she asked, already afraid she knew the answer.

"You've never been to Juan Carlos before? They have the best tacos and freshly made pico de gallo in the entire state of California," he responded without actually answering her question.

She prayed for patience. "Please tell me that the important business meeting that you required I accompany you to isn't sitting at the bar and stuffing your face with tacos?"

"Well, it won't just be tacos. There will be pico de gallo. And rice pudding or flan depending on my mood. Believe me when I say it will be a step up from the stuffy office Christmas party that I've rescued you from."

"Are you completely out of your mind? I barely have enough time in the day as it is, trying to get these responses filed, putting together the PowerPoint presentation for next week's meeting with the board on the EAP proposal, not to mention reviewing the latest round of contract proposals from the Blossom group."

He drew his face into a serious expression, his lips almost pouty. "Duly noted. But besides escaping the dreary office party, we did manage to finalize those responses and drew up a tentative schedule for the management training that you're going to be heading up."

All true. Not to mention that, by slipping out, she'd fended off Mike from Marketing's attempt to corner her to discuss some of his personal legal issues that had nothing to do with his job. And he wasn't alone, as more and more members of the executive level were trying to bum some free legal advice off her. Last week she'd counseled Fran from IT about whether she should fight an HOA fine after her dog crapped on the rug in the foyer.

But as time-consuming as it could be, she had to admit there was something invigorating about having the trust of so many people in such a short amount of time. She felt valued.

Or played, depending how you looked at it.

She sighed, her silence her concession.

"Besides," James continued, "we're already here. We

might as well take advantage of the opportunity to try one of Juan Carlos's tacos."

She glanced at her watch. Nearly one o'clock. "Fine, but you have one hour and then we're out of here."

He grabbed her hand and pulled her up from the car. A simple gesture for some and one that James had undoubtedly done hundreds of times with the scores of women in his life.

Only Quinn wasn't used to such handling, and her hand was tingling where he held it.

But this was James Thornhill, she reminded herself. A man who'd told her just yesterday that a five percent pay increase to thousands of hardworking employees who'd been working at the same salary for the past three years despite the increased cost of living was out of the question. A man who'd just spent an unknown amount of money flying to San Diego in a privately owned company jet to eat tacos.

Like she'd told her friends, she was not and never, ever would be interested in a man like that, no matter how her traitorous body superficially reacted to his obvious charms.

Case closed.

TWO TACOS LOADED WITH CHEESE, sour cream, and guacamole, a pound of chips and salsa, and half of James's rice pudding later, Quinn leaned back in the booth and groaned while James tried not to laugh at her misery.

Who'd have guessed such a slight woman like Quinn Taylor could put so much food away? Every meal he shared with her was an experience, one he looked forward to.

Actually, it was always like that with Quinn. In the past

month since she'd come to work with him, he'd learned to rely on her insight in almost every decision he made. She was smart, hardworking, and reliable to a fault. Not to mention funny—sometimes unintentionally—quirky, and quickly becoming indispensable.

"You know, they make a pretty good fried ice cream if you want to give it a go."

She moaned, and this time he did laugh.

"Jimmy!"

James smiled as the older man somewhere in his mid-fifties came over to greet him. Juan Carlos, the proprietor of the joint and one of James's oldest friends.

"You should have told me you would be coming today. I would have had Elena prepare your special dish."

"We just happened to be in the area and thought we'd grab something to eat."

Quinn raised her brows at that outright lie but didn't say anything.

"And who's the lovely lady?" Juan asked, turning his attention to her.

"Quinn just joined us at Thornhill," James said. "She's our new in-house employment attorney."

"Ah, very good to meet you, Quinn. I think you'll find that most employees acquainted with Jimmy here are usually fairly happy in their employment."

"You used to work for the company and...Jimmy?" she asked, her voice brimming with laughter. She glanced at him, not trying to hide her amusement.

She looked good when she smiled.

"Jimmy and I both used to be line cooks at the Silver Grill," Juan said, patting him on the back.

Quinn couldn't hide the shock from her voice. "Line

cooks? With…Jimmy?" She waved her hand at him as if Juan had been confused with the question.

Juan chuckled. "*Sí*, not that he was very good at first. Burned everything. But a few weeks under my tutelage and he was almost half as good as me."

"You see, Quinn," James said and reached over to beat her to the last chip that he'd watched her eying for the past few minutes, "I am a man of many hidden talents."

"Right."

While James took a few more minutes to catch up with Juan, it was hard to ignore the curious expression on Quinn's face as she studied him, likely still trying to get her head around the fact that he'd once worked in the kitchen at one of his grandfather's restaurants.

"Could I get a refill of my soda?" she asked their waitress when she returned and set their ticket on the table.

Juan appeared outraged. "You know your money isn't good here, Jimmy. Leah, comp their ticket—"

But James had already reached for the tab. "I think we both know I'm good for it."

"You would do me a great disservice if you didn't let me have the honor of feeding you. After all, none of this would be possible if not for you."

James met the man's eyes for a second. "Fine, if you feel that strongly about it. But next time you're up north, I'm paying."

Satisfied, Juan nodded and the men clasped hands before he turned to her. "It was lovely to meet you, Quinn."

Showing restraint, since James had a fair idea of the millions of questions she probably was dying to ask his good friend Juan, Quinn smiled and shook his hand.

"Okay. Spill," she said the moment the car door shut behind them. He hadn't thought she'd make it to the car.

"What on earth were *you* doing working as a line cook? I imagine your weekly allowance would have been as much as some people make in a year."

A prospect that James would have campaigned for if he had thought it would do him any good. But the money he was left after his parents died when he was eight was held in a trust until he was twenty-one, leaving his grandfather as his sole means of support. Not that the old man was tight, but he wanted James to learn a certain level of fiscal responsibility growing up.

"I have my grandfather to thank for that. He wanted me to understand what a day of hard work really meant rather than just hand over money for me to do as I liked. So instead of hanging out in Europe or the beaches of Mexico with my friends, I was busting my balls for two summers, working my way around the kitchen."

The fact that she didn't ask him anything about why his grandfather played such a role in his life told James that Quinn had probably done her research and already knew the old man had raised him since he was eight. Instead, she asked, "What does Juan have to be grateful to you for?"

"You know. Stuff," he said vaguely. "Now, by my estimate, we still have another thirty minutes before we have to leave to stay on your schedule, and there's this great bakery where we could pick up—"

"You have to be kidding. You could eat? But don't be changing the subject. What did you do for Juan?" she persisted.

He sighed, knowing there was no use avoiding the question. "A few years ago, Juan was looking for some investors to help him expand his business. He wanted to open up two more restaurants but needed the capital to get them going. He opened his second and most profitable restaurant—this one—four years ago today. He was actually our first successful investment. As I see it, contrary to his belief, we owe each other."

"Ah. Back when you were a venture capitalist. That must have been risky for you. Going out on a limb like that for a friend."

"Not at all. As I suspected, the investment was sound, and he's now expanding operations farther north. Juan Carlos has been very profitable for our investors. Well, I should say, the firm's investors. I stepped down when I became CEO of Thornhill."

"And what are you going to do when your grandfather is ready to return to the helm? Will you go back?"

Leave it to Quinn to always ask the hard questions.

When the board approached him to take on this position, there was an unspoken possibility that, with his grandfather's age and decreasing health, the position might turn into something more permanent. But it wasn't something he'd talked to his grandfather about yet, and now, with the old man just out of the hospital barely a month and recovering at home, it also wasn't something James was ready to broach.

And he also wasn't yet ready to talk about it.

"I don't really know. I like to keep my options open." He grinned, appearing for all purposes as a wanderlust, aimless guy—something he'd perfected over the years.

Quinn didn't look surprised, her lips pursing in disapproval.

"Hey. The board is an antiquated group of old men who like things how they've been done for decades, so with me and my new crazy ideas—like bringing you on and rallying for the EAP thing—they're probably just waiting for me to fail." Kind of the story of his life. "So it's very possible I could be out on my ass by the end of the year."

"Maybe. But for what it's worth, I think what you're doing, the energy and ideas you're bringing, are progressive and much needed."

"You would, of course. Since your little employee-assistance plan is one of them. You know, that bakery shop I was mentioning isn't all that far from here."

"We just ate a mountain of food. How could you even have room?"

"Come on, you forget that I know you. And I'm betting that a double chocolate salted caramel brownie would really hit the spot."

She was practically salivating at his mention of the word *chocolate*, but rather than agree immediately as most sane people would, Quinn scowled. One thing the woman hated more than his teasing was being predictable. And he totally had her number.

He considered another approach. "You did mention that it was your friend's birthday, so it wouldn't hurt for us to take a look, maybe find some sort of cake that you could buy her."

She was considering it, he could tell as she pushed her monstrous glasses higher up on her nose. "All right. I guess we could just check out the place. But no dallying around, James. I need to get back."

He held his hand up. "I promise. No dallying."

Anything to keep the woman's company for a little longer before they returned to the responsibilities waiting for them back at the office.

4

"WHAT DID you tell your family about why you're not making it home for Christmas?" Anna shouted over the club music playing near fever-pitch level later that same night. The place was one of Anna's favorites, even if Tessa and Quinn were less enthusiastic, thanks to the meat-market vibe of the place.

"The truth," Quinn hollered, hoping her voice would hold out till the end of the night. "That I'm just too swamped to try and get away from work right now. Especially with this Blossom deal still being hammered out and the EAP proposal to put together."

"You are going to drive up to the farmhouse on Christmas Eve with Anna and me, though. Right?" Tess asked. "You can't spend Christmas day alone."

"Of course." She and Anna had been to Tessa's family home for Christmas for three of the past five Christmases. Something made necessary when time constraints and budget made it impossible to make it home. "There are no people I'd rather spend the holidays with."

"Hear, hear," Anna said and held up her martini before

taking a drink. For Anna, getting away to the farm was a welcome relief from a lonely meal alone on those holidays anyhow. Her mother was an anthropology professor at Berkeley and was usually off conducting field studies of some aboriginal tribe in South America or the burial rituals of a sub-Saharan clan in Africa during the holidays.

"How'd Sabrina take the news you weren't coming home?" Tess asked.

Quinn's younger sister had been less understanding about her bailing on Christmas, something Quinn couldn't blame her for, what with moving back home a couple years before to help with their mom. She could probably use a break from the parental focus. Fortunately, Quinn had laid out a plan to help appease Sabrina, which included spearheading and footing the bill on the surprise party for her parents' upcoming thirtieth anniversary party they were throwing in February. Come hell or high water, Quinn would make sure to be there for that big event.

A bored-looking waitress arrived with a round of shots and placed them on their table. "From the table in the corner."

Quinn glanced over to see a couple of guys grinning at them. Shaking her head, she shared a look with Tessa. "Record time. We've been here less than five minutes and she already got us our next order of drinks."

"Why do you think it's all about me?" Anna asked and passed the shots around the table. "With your creamy-white Irish skin and those black curls," she said to Tessa before turning to Quinn, "and your tall, svelte Ice Queen thing, they could very well have been meant for either of you. I mean, your headband alone is enough to inspire plenty of X-rated fantasies."

Almost self-consciously, Quinn's hand went to her hair,

smoothing it down over her shoulders. "Hey, it's keeping my hair from my eyes, especially since you've forbidden me from stepping foot inside this place with a ponytail, bun, or any such variation."

"And since when do you listen to me?" Anna shot back playfully. "Considering I've begged you to consider wearing your contacts so you can stop hiding behind those glasses that are big enough to fit Frankenstein."

"Hey. I like my glasses."

"You like *hiding* behind your glasses."

"That's not true. Besides, I think wearing them adds a certain aura of authority. You try speaking to a fifty-eight year old guy who thinks you're just a five-foot seven Kewpie Doll."

"Uh-huh. Right. And why are you still wearing them?" Anna persisted.

"The smoke bothers my eyes."

Her friends both laughed. "You do realize there's no smoking in here," Tessa said.

"It drifts in from outside."

"Well, if we're going to hope for another round, we need to chug these down, ladies," Anna said.

Tessa held hers up and Quinn joined her. "To Anna on her twenty-eight birthday. To new adventures."

"And shaking that damn gossip beat," Anna added before throwing hers back.

Quinn threw hers back and was just swallowing the fiery liquid when she saw someone across the room whose presence sent her choking and her eyes watering.

Anna laughed, pounding her back. "You sure are a lightweight."

"It's not that," she said, still staring in disbelief. "Over there."

Anna and Tessa glanced over to the bar, where a group of women were fawning all over Thornhill Management's CEO, who didn't appear to mind.

"Is that...?" Tess asked.

"If you mean my boss, then yes."

Anna whistled under her breath. "He sure is easy on the eyes. And you get to stare at that mug every day? No wonder you work so many late nights at the office."

"Not funny." Quinn picked up her rum and Coke and took a sip. "I guess he's kind of good-looking, in that over-privileged, inbred way. But frankly, I don't even notice." Not much.

"Sure you don't," Anna said, not giving up.

Almost as if his ears were burning from their conversation, James glanced over, pausing mid-sentence as his eyes locked on hers. There was a light of recognition in his eyes, and his lips quirked up in that enticing way of his. "Oh, God. He's coming over."

Had she just yelled that?

From her friends' laughter, she was going to guess yes. That shot must be hitting her faster than she'd have expected, if her body's sudden increase in temperature were any indication.

"Don't let me say anything embarrassing— Wait. Don't *you* guys dare say anything embarrassing," Quinn corrected.

Anna took a playful sip of her martini and smiled. "No promises."

"Good evening, ladies," James said in that familiar way that told her he'd greeted many women in the same fashion. With the same grin.

Whatever you do, Quinn, don't look directly at him or his—

"Quinn, fancy meeting you here tonight. You're not stalking me or something, are you?"

She whipped her head toward him.

Damn. He got her. And why, dear Lord in heaven, why did he have to wear such a form-fitting shirt that displayed every ripple of muscle? Was there something wrong with an ordinary turtleneck?

She shook her head. No. He couldn't be here. Not when her defenses were down, and definitely not when he was wearing anything other than the uniform suit and tie from the office.

"Don't be ridiculous. Why would I be stalking you, if anything I should ask—"

She stopped when she saw him wink at Anna and Tessa, who were barely holding back their laughter.

Right, he was kidding. Where had her sense of humor gone?"

"And who might you be?" Anna asked, sounding almost convincing in not knowing him.

"Oh. James, this is Anna and Tessa," she said pointing to each woman. "And this is James Thornhill, my boss."

"Nice to meet you ladies. I'd offer to buy you all a round of drinks, but it appears you've already got it covered," he said as the waitress returned with another round of shots that she set down.

Quinn sensed him studying her again, but she couldn't trust herself to meet those eyes. Not when it felt like he and everyone in the place could read everything crossing her mind.

"Well, I didn't mean to interrupt your festivities. I just thought I'd stop and say hello."

She lifted her hand and gave a quick wave before sucking down the rum and Coke.

"Nice meeting you," Anna and Tessa echoed, not hiding the fact they were watching him walk away with appreciative grins.

"He seems nice. Not like the spawn of Satan at all," Tessa said.

"The verdict is still out."

"Should we have another toast, then?" Anna asked, already raising her shot glass.

"I'm out," Quinn said, studying the dark liquid dubiously. "No way can I show up tomorrow nursing a hangover." Plus, having her boss just several yards away with a harem of women hanging on his every word made the whole night suddenly awkward.

"Two shots will not give you a hangover. Come on, just one more, pretty please?" Anna cajoled. "Then, since I can see you already have your 'how can I escape' face on, now that you've spied your boss, we can hit the club across the way for some dancing."

"Hey, if I can do it despite an early morning in court tomorrow on a property dispute, so can you," Tessa said and held her shot glass up.

One more shot and they could leave, no begging required? That she could do.

"Fine. Last one, then I'm on water the rest of the night."

With a quick glance to make sure James wasn't watching her debauchery—which she didn't have to worry about since he was completely enraptured by whatever the barely twenty-one-year-old girl was saying—she threw it back.

JAMES TOOK a seat on the couch across from his grandfather, whose home nurse buzzed around, trying to make sure he had everything he needed. James was surprised to see the old man let anyone help him for a change without his scaring them away. But Jenny was already somewhere in her mid-fifties and didn't seem to scare easily, something that his grandfather needed. A firm hand from someone as stubborn as him.

"Thanks, Jenny," Cyrus Thornhill said, which seemed to be the signal she needed to clear the room.

"I'll be back with your meds in fifteen," she said in warning before leaving them alone.

James glanced at his watch, calculating the minutes until he could make his excuses to leave. Ordinarily he left immediately after Sunday dinner, a tradition his grandfather had insisted on when James was growing up, and that, when Cyrus left the hospital a month before, they'd resumed again. But it was Christmas, and James felt he owed the man the courtesy of staying, even if he didn't feel particularly wanted.

"Dinner was great. It's too bad that Uncle Walter and his family couldn't join us this year."

"Maybe next year." Cyrus picked up a glass of water, flinching as he drank it. "What I wouldn't give to have a glass of brandy right now."

Brandy was usually the old man's preferred Sunday after-dinner drink, but since his heart attack, he was strictly forbidden from drinking the stuff—or any alcohol for that matter. Something that his nurse had taken to heart and hidden every drop of alcohol in the house, according to Cyrus when James came to see him right after he'd left the hospital. The old man had since come to terms with it, no longer berating the harried nurse.

"You're looking much better," James said, noticing the color had returned to Cyrus's face and he was walking a lot taller again, whereas before he was like a shadow as he moved around—when he moved at all.

"I'm doing all right." He turned his attention to James, studying him. "So, I had an interesting phone call the other day. Dennis wanted to fill me in on a few things that were going on."

James gritted his teeth. Every change he was trying to make within the company, was meeting a wall of interference in the form of one Dennis Monson. "Contrary to what Dennis might have told you, our discussion with the Blossom Brew folk is going great. In fact, I'm meeting with a number of banks next week to secure the financing for the franchise, and once we have that in place, it's just a matter of signing the contracts and moving onto the next stage."

"All well and good, but that isn't what we talked about. Dennis seems to think this new gal, this attorney you brought in, is stirring up trouble with her ideas of adding more insurance assistance to employees, not to mention mandating time-consuming legal training for managers that no one has time for. We're in the business of running restaurants, something many of our managers have been doing since well before you were in diapers."

Which was precisely part of the problem.

But first things first. Quinn had been working late every night, her dedication to improving the working environment for the employees something to be commended, not ridiculed, which was precisely what Dennis had been doing. Undermining her, not to mention undermining James. He'd have fired him on the spot a month ago but there were too many on the board still loyal to him. Including his grandfather.

"Quinn Taylor is hardly stirring up trouble," he said, forcing his tone to sound even and calm. "You've said it yourself, that the strength and success in any company relies in the strength and success of its employees. If you'd seen the PowerPoint presentation she gave on this to the board a couple days ago, you would have seen that the upfront cost to us to provide this employee assistance plan is minimal, while the benefits it could provide those employees who might need it, would be significant."

Cyrus nodded, grim faced. "And the training? Our managers are already stretched thin enough. Dennis tells me you want to require all upper level managers take her legal classes. Isn't that a bit much?"

"Definitely not. Hell, more than half of our upper level management are over fifty and have no idea that they can't just tell a pregnant server they're cutting their hours because they don't want to risk harming the baby, or that they can't just fire an employee when they find out they have epilepsy. If there's one thing I've learned since knowing Quinn, is that we have a legal and ethical obligation to make sure we're doing our best to provide a safe and legally compliant workplace for *all* our employees."

"Wow. That's quite the speech, James. I'm surprised you care so much to be this invested."

"Why wouldn't I be invested? I agreed to take on your role until you're better. And that's what I'm doing, while trying to implement changes that will help Thornhill Management thrive and grow in the coming years."

"I think you might believe that. For now. Or until the next shining new business idea takes hold and you jump ship, leaving all these lofty plans in someone else's hands to implement."

Why did James even try? It was always the same. "If you had such little trust in me and my dedication to the company, why did you go along with the board's decision to bring me on?"

"Lying up in a hospital bed with a million tubes stuck in me, I didn't see I had a lot of choice. Come now, James. Don't act so outraged that I would be cautious. This from the boy who two weeks after he started drum lessons decided he wanted to try the sax. Who tried rugby until he decided that lacrosse would be a better fit. Who changed his major three times before finally committing and graduating with one. Not to mention the number of start ups you've given up on over the years."

Of course, that would be how his grandfather saw things. Not that, when James did commit to Lacrosse, he and his team took all-state two times in a year and he was named the league's MVP. Or that despite changing his mind on his major in the first year of school—when kids typically are exploring what they wanted—he ultimately graduated summa cum laude with a business degree from Princeton. Or that for the previous four years before he came back to Thornhill, he'd successfully started his own company, personally overseeing the investment and growth in the small mom and pop shops that he provided capital for, until he grew his company into a multi-billion dollar success.

No, James would always be seen as an aimless kid who couldn't decide between the drums or the sax.

The only way James could prove himself to his grandfather was to make everything he had been busting his butt to build over the past month happen. No, not just happen, but also be wildly successful.

"I'm sorry that you always see me as a disappointment. But I promise that you're going to see significant return on our investment in the coming months and years. Not just with the Blossom deal, but also the added legal training that will protect our bottom dollar when we defend against lawsuits. When our employees know that they're working for a company that cares about all their health needs, physical *and mental.*"

"I guess time will tell, son." There was an odd light in his grandfather's blue eyes as he continued to study James for a minute, a light James couldn't decipher before Cyrus closed his eyes, suddenly appearing all of his seventy-two years. "Actually, maybe you can call Jenny for me. Today has worn me out more than I thought and I want to retire to my room."

James stood, feeling a bit battered and weary himself. "Of course. I hope you'll be feeling better."

"That makes two of us. Merry Christmas."

Later that night, James stood for a moment in the entranceway of his penthouse apartment where he was scheduled to be hosting a small party of thirty people in the next hour. The whole place felt empty. Lonely.

More than twenty years ago, not long after he'd waited on that cold rainy day for his parents who would never show up for his big soccer game because they'd been killed en route in a pile up on the interstate, James had promised himself never to open himself to that kind of pain again.

And not just the pain. But the anger, the helplessness, and the terror that came from loving people who could just so easily be taken away from you.

He'd lived his live from then on, not committing to much of anything except having a good time, doing what felt right in the moment, and breaking things off just when he felt himself liking it just a little too much. This included relationships with women, friends, jobs, and even pets.

Up to now, he'd been happy with that decision. Well, happy enough. He had more than enough money to buy the things he wanted, the health to do the things he aspired to do, and the balls to give anything a try at least once, no matter the risk.

But lately, he'd been finding a sort of hollowness to his life. The parties, the women, the thrill of trying new things, weren't as fulfilling as they had once been.

He thought about his grandfather who, having lost his wife, and then his son and daughter-in-law, built up a wall around him, not letting anyone in—not even eight-year old James. And he had seemed content enough, focusing his energy in his business. His legacy, as he'd once told James. Only now, as he sat up in his room alone in that big house, James wondered whether the old man had any regrets. Did he wish that maybe he had let people in, tried to live his life differently?

Or was he wondering, like James, if closing himself off from caring was more lonely and unbearable than if he'd taken a chance and opened himself to love again?

A knock on the door behind him brought James from his thoughts. The caterers had arrived, ready to set up for the night, and in the bustle of preparation, James was happy to push aside the questions that he'd been pondering, needing a little frivolity and merriment to remind himself of why he did it all.

Briefly, he wondered what Quinn might be doing at that moment.

He knew that instead of heading home to Idaho for the holiday, she and her roommates had escaped to Tessa's family farm up in Sonoma. And even though she was probably having a great time sharing a dinner, maybe drinking eggnog by the fireside, he felt guilty that he hadn't helped her find the time to be with her family. He knew well how fleeting life could be.

He was going to have to make it up to her. Because in the past few weeks, they'd become more than just boss and employee. They'd become friends. Good friends. And to that end—and that end alone, he sharply reminded himself—he wanted to see her happiness ensured. It was the least he could do after everything she was doing for him, for his vision.

Next time she made plans to see her family, he was going to make sure she kept that promise. Because you never knew whether, in the next moment, it could all be taken away from you.

5

"YOU SHOULD HAVE SEEN Dennis's face when the board voted to approve the financing, despite his concerns," James said, his eyes shining with laughter as he shoved a bloody piece of steak in his mouth.

It was two weeks since the New Year and Quinn and James were enjoying their usual Wednesday lunch. James's spirits were higher than they'd been in the days after Christmas, when he'd seemed a little pensive, almost sad, something that was completely unlike him. It was good to see him finding his joy of life again, especially if it meant at Dennis's expense.

"Well, congratulations," she said, picking up her Coke Zero and draining the last of it through the straw. "You've worked so hard to get everything to this point. Although, I don't understand why Thornhill Management needs to come up with twenty percent capital if you're getting this investment bank to lend the company the money to secure the franchise."

He shrugged. "It's standard. Crestwood Bank is fronting a substantial sum to make this work and they, like any other bank, want to see that we have some skin in the game. But the board's approval today? I can't tell you how long I've been sweating this. If there was one thing I thought that might hold us up, it was this. It's one thing to get on board with adding a new, possibly high profiting franchise, another thing to have to cough up a significant sum to support it."

"This is definitely going to make the next few weeks smoother as we get to the end of closing the deal with the Blossom group. I want this thing settled and put to bed before I go on vacation next month."

"Vacation?" James asked.

"I've told you three times. My parents' anniversary party? The one I'm supposed to be planning for half the town? My sister will hire a hit man if I miss this."

"Oh, right. That sounds familiar. Well, I assure you, this thing will be wrapped up all nice and tidy with a bow before you're on the flight to Bazooka."

"Eureka," she said, stabbing an artichoke heart. "Eureka, Idaho."

"That's what I said."

She rolled her eyes. "Of course you did. Now, where were things left with the EAP? They were supposed to be voting on that next week."

"Yes, well"—James took a drink of water—"It's coming. You have to understand, with these people, it has to be one thing at a time. Especially when we're asking them to do something that will affect the bottom line. Profits. Give me a couple more weeks, and we'll bring it to a vote. Just like with this Blossom deal, and your legal training, they had to warm up to each idea at their own time."

Quinn tried not to get frustrated. There were a lot of things happening, a lot of changes, and she couldn't expect it to happen at once. Progress was coming, it was just coming a little slower than she liked. Such as the legal training that officially got off the ground this past week. And for all their complaints and condescension of not needing it, she had been rewarded when a handful of them came up to her at the end to say how much they'd learned that would help them in their daily operations.

Not to say there weren't still a few holdouts. Like Paul, her former client's old boss. He was supposed to have come to yesterday's session but had found himself conveniently called away. He of all people needed it most of all.

"How is everything for you, Mr. Thornhill?" their server asked, appearing at James's side. The girl—because, come on, she didn't look older than twelve—was a tad overly attentive, especially when it came to making sure that James had everything he wanted. A trait Quinn discovered wasn't uncommon whenever they went out.

"Everything is excellent, isn't that right, Quinn?"

"Yeah, sure. Can I get another Coke Zero, please?"

"You know, Kimberly, I think I might have room for one of those chocolate soufflés today," James said, using the server's name as he always did when they went to a restaurant. Makes them feel valued and appreciated, he'd told her when she asked him about it. "Would you mind having one of those thrown in for us now?"

"Sure thing. I'll be back to check on you in a few minutes," Kimberly said and scurried away.

"I'll bet you will," Quinn said under her breath.

James glanced at her. "What? Don't you like Kimberly? I thought she was a sweet girl. Very attentive."

Quinn snorted. "I'll say. James, do you think it's possible for you to go one meal without getting the phone number of whatever adolescent who serves us?"

"Sorry to shatter your illusions, but I only get the number from women over twenty-one." He shoveled in another bite of steak. "Besides, a little friendliness goes a long way."

"Flirtation and friendliness are not the same thing," she said, looking around for any sign of Kimberly and that promised glass of Coke Zero.

"Well, you certainly weren't complaining when my friendliness earned us an extra basket of cheesy bread the other day at Pizza Haven. Or when Danielle from Marco's threw in the extra piece of chocolate cheesecake that you devoured in less than three minutes. Actually, Quinn, you might find that you get more out of life with honey than you do with vinegar."

"Just because I don't flirt with everyone who breathes and passes in my vicinity doesn't mean I'm being...vinegary. Come to think of it, *you* might do with some legal training yourself. Brush up on a few things about sexual harassment and hostile work environment."

He raised his brows. "Are you seriously concerned that, when you're looking the other way, I'm busy sexually harassing my assistant, good old Pauline?"

"No, not because you sexually harass your secretary. But because you just said good *old* Pauline."

He laughed. "I'll give it some thought." Reaching across to her plate, James spearheaded one of the disgusting black olives she had pushed aside to the corner of her plate. "Did you ever give that real estate fellow of mine a call?"

Quinn picked up her glass and drained the last of the contents, then shook the ice trying to get a little more fluid to sink to the bottom of the glass. "I decided that, for the time being, I'm just going to stay where I am. I like my roommates, and I'd hate for them to spend time finding a new roommate who flakes out on them when it's time to pay the rent, leaving them in the lurch."

"Sure. Or could it be you have the tiniest bit of concern that they might just be replacing you?"

"That's ridiculous," she said, her laugh coming more forced than natural. She would never be so insecure as to worry about something like that. Just because some other unknown woman would be there plopped down on their couch eating pizza and drinking wine on those late nights where someone just needed to talk, or sitting in her seat at the breakfast table when Tessa served up her famous cinnamon rolls every Sunday morning, didn't have to mean she was being replaced. "I haven't even given that any thought."

From the look he gave her, she didn't think she'd convinced him. "Whatever you say. You do realize, when I sent you Rich's number, you were supposed to call him not just because you needed a realtor, but maybe because you were going to give the guy a chance and go out with him?"

"Rich." She looked incredulously at him. "Rich, the guy you introduced me to last week at the Thai place? Rich, the guy with the comb-over and the high laugh who thinks that the Macarena was the greatest dance movement of the twentieth century?" Then there was the most unforgiving of all. "And who, I might add, didn't even vote in the last Presidential race. Nope. No way. He's most definitely not my type."

James grabbed the ketchup bottle, squirting a torrent of the condiment over his plate of fries. "Okay. Then before I try and set you up with the next poor guy, why don't you tell me a little about who is your type? Maybe start with your last boyfriend. What was his name?"

"I don't need you to set me up with anyone, James. I'm

perfectly capable of finding my own dates, thank you very much."

He looked skeptical. "When was the last time you went on a date? And I don't mean when you went for a coffee with the guy who unplugged the kitchen drain last week."

She tried to remember, almost certain she'd gone out at some point in the past few weeks. Must have been before the New Year, okay, maybe before Christmas, or had it been...

"Fine. It's been a while since I dated. And his name was Chuck. Your point?"

James choked on his drink. "Chuck as in chuck steak? Chuck wagon? Chuck the giant murderous doll? Chuck like—"

"Yes, James. Chuck. Can we grow up a little? You're the one who asked."

"You're quite right. So what was Chuck like? What did he do for a living?"

"He was an actuary."

His shoulders shook suspiciously. "An actuary? As in one of those guys who calculates risk into a quantifiable number for insurance purposes? Wow. He must have been quite adventurous."

"Okay, I knew I shouldn't have said anything."

"I'm sorry. Please. Continue. What kind of man was Chuck the actuary?"

She rearranged the lettuce on her plate with her fork, taking a moment to answer. "He was really quite nice. Maybe not exactly adventurous, but then again, neither am I. We can't all be thrill seekers who like cliff diving in Costa Rica or traipsing through the Australian outback."

"Those were all just as educational as they were fun," he

said. "So aside from both of you enjoying not-adventurous things, did you really like this guy, this Chuck?"

She avoided meeting his eyes. "Of course. He was nice. Sweet. Good-looking in an understated way."

"Hardly a ringing endorsement," he said dryly. "Maybe tell me about the last guy you went out with that you actually really cared about. That you were head-over-heels in love with."

She was not about to go there. "You know, if anyone needs their love life dissected around here, James, it's you. I mean, how many women can you possibly date in one night? Wait, don't answer that. Maybe the better question isn't how many women *can* you date, but how many *should* you date in one night? There is something to be said for quality over quantity."

"I'm sure you make a valid point, but I can't think of any reason why getting to know as many beautiful women as I can is a bad thing. Sure, maybe some of them aren't as cultured or as smart as the others."

"James, your last date thought the Alamo was a country-western band. Maybe you could strive a little harder—" She paused as her cell phone chirped and she glanced down. "Shoot. I have a meeting with a couple of managers in ten minutes to review some accommodation procedures." She dropped her napkin on the table and shook the ice in her glass again, trying to get a last swallow.

"You're still going to tour those properties with me and the Blossom Brew group later this evening?"

She was typing something on her phone, not yet looking up. "I can," she said, typing in a message to Jeanne that she was a few minutes behind, "But isn't Dennis more than capable of answering any questions they may have?"

"Answering them, I suppose. Answering them in a way

that doesn't outright sabotage this deal I can't say. Which is why I would prefer to have someone around that I can trust."

"Right. Just call me your Girl Friday." She sighed. "I guess I can tell the girls I won't be able to make it to the new Tina Fey movie after all. I don't need a life outside of work, right?"

"You have a life," he countered. "Just last week I took you to the Seattle Mariners game. You had a hot dog, some nachos. And even laughed a time or two, if memory serves."

"How could I forget." She came to her feet. "I'll see you back at the office."

"You really have to leave? Can't you reschedule? I just ordered us a chocolate soufflé."

She looked into his hopeful blue eyes framed beautifully by the darkness of his lashes, the easy smile that tugged at his lips... "You can save me a bite."

With relief at having an excuse to get away from James and his prying questions and his all-knowing eyes, she scooped her red handbag off the seat next to her and, with a wave, headed out.

At the door, she stopped, taking a moment to look back at the table where Kimberly had returned and was fawning all over James. The woman had probably been waiting for Quinn to leave. James smiled like he always did and sipped his drink while she talked. Although she'd given him grief about his flirting, she knew that most of the time he was being polite, not wanting to hurt the women's feelings. James tended to prefer his women a little older and more worldly. Which didn't really help the strange feeling in the pit of her stomach that had been becoming more and more regular.

A small sigh pulled at the back of her throat.

Wait. Where'd that come from?

Before James could spot her spying, Quinn turned and raced out the door. Had she really been considering, even for a minute, putting off her meeting so she could share dessert with James?

It was one thing these past few weeks to have suddenly found herself wanting to look her best—or at least less like a prude and more like the young semi-attractive woman she knew she could be—and another thing to consider blowing off work to put herself under the spell of James Thornhill any more than she had to.

James was her boss.

Quinn would never date her boss under any circumstance, least of all when she was just months away from paying off the last of her mom's medical bills. Not to mention that said boss was a womanizing philanderer allergic to any romantic commitment that lasted longer than a common cold.

Then there was the fact that he would never in a million years find anyone as ordinary as her as dating material.

But knowing all of this didn't help ease the conflict she was struggling with of late.

Quinn waved to James's driver but kept walking, needing the few blocks to the office to clear her head. Fortunately, it was a warmer-than-average afternoon in San Francisco for January, and she had her jacket to ward off any chill.

What she'd told James, about feeling like she'd become his Girl Friday, was more than just a flippant remark. Their growing codependency was the reason she couldn't go an hour—awake or asleep—without some passing thought that involved the guy.

After all, they'd spent nearly fifteen hours a day almost six days a week together since she'd started. She was bound to become delusional, what with the lack of regular interaction with any other man—or person, for that matter.

Her roommates already had been hinting that she spent more time with James than either of them in the entire previous year. Which was precisely why this break, this mini-vacation back home next month, was so needed. She had to get away from his influence. She needed to see that she could exist outside of James Thornhill's sphere.

Something that seemed almost unthinkable the more time she spent with the man.

6

"THIS IS INSANE," Quinn said, pacing James's office three weeks later.

She stared at the most recent amendment to the agreement with Blossom Brew that was supposed to have been finalized that morning. Unbelievable. "Why do they keep bringing up these ridiculous points?" She stared at the clock before smacking her head with her palm. "My flight leaves in an hour. There's no way I'm going to make it."

"Relax, Quinn. It's going to work out. You'll see," James said, throwing the tennis ball against the wall and catching it, as he'd been doing for the past ten minutes. "I'm supposed to be heading to Cabo San Lucas this very minute, and you don't see me getting my knickers in a twist."

"Easy for you to say. You don't have a mile-long list of things to get done before seventy-five people are scheduled to arrive at the Elks Building in downtown Eureka in two days' time while you're still stuck nine hundred miles away."

Not to mention the fact that, in that thin dark cashmere sweater the same color as his eyes, Quinn was finding it hard not to just sink into their blue depths. Yep. She really needed to get away. STAT.

"Why, again, are you insisting that I give the final approval on these contracts? Dennis is more than capable." It was something she'd said more than a hundred times over the past few weeks.

He stared at her in disbelief. "You know why. You're more aware than anyone how Dennis would sooner see the company implode than see this deal succeed."

James was right, which meant that she was going to be royally screwed when it came to honoring her promise, once again, to her sister. There was a knock on the door a second before Jeannie came in, carrying the information Quinn had asked for. Quinn read through the document, trying to concentrate on the numbers as James threw the ball again and again and again until, unable to take the torture, she went over and caught it midair.

James started to object but thought better of it when he caught sight of her face. A moment later, with assurances she was scanning everything and faxing the signatures again to their investors, Jeannie hurried out.

Quinn's phone buzzed and she glanced down. Four missed text messages. Two from her sister, Sabrina, and one from each of her roommates wishing her a safe flight.

At this rate, there wouldn't be a flight.

"The parents checking to see if you're on your way?"

"Hardly." She dropped the phone back down before collapsing on the small leather couch situated under the windows of James's office. "They don't know I'm arriving. It's supposed to be part of the surprise. Surprise arrival, surprise anniversary party? Remember? But I suppose if Mom and Dad don't know I'm coming, they won't be disappointed when I never arrive. My sister, however, is another story."

He chuckled and leaned forward, tapping something on his keyboard. Quinn looked over to find that, while she was going nearly bald from pulling her hair out to get everything finalized, the CEO and supposed head engineer of the whole deal was posting something witty on his Facebook wall.

She bolted upright, her nerves stretched to the breaking point. "I don't get you, James. On one hand, you present this image of a man who wants to bring the company that his grandfather started into the twenty-first century. A man who wants to work hard to see the company succeed and grow, hold a commanding presence to the board members and convince them that things are really going to get better. Then at other times you're still acting like a rich, spoiled, aimless player who would rather be teeing off or flying to a getaway in Cabo instead of commanding the ship. Like you can't decide where you want to be. In the meantime, I'm killing myself to get everything done." She caught her breath, surprised she'd had so much to say.

"You're that worried about catching this flight then?" he asked, nonplussed by her speech.

She threw her hands up. "Of course I am. Haven't you been listening? I have to catch a flight to Seattle and then Spokane, where I'll rent a car and drive more than seventy-five miles to Eureka, a drive that I vastly prefer to do when there's daylight and the skies are clear—not at ten o'clock at night when there's a winter storm watch for the area."

"You do realize, of course, that I have access to a small, private aircraft that can take you anywhere you need to go? I'm sure that if I talk it over with my pilot, we could arrange a slight detour on our way to Mexico and drop you off in... Idaho, is it?"

Quinn forced herself to count to ten before responding. "It's one thing for you to just up and take a flight to wherever you want and claim a tax write-off for whatever reason—"

"Mental health check."

"—but it's another thing entirely for me to let you abuse your corporate write-offs on my account. Further, I could never accept such a generous offer. It would be highly inappropriate."

"Why not? You're missing your current flight because you're trying to complete this business deal. Why shouldn't I, at the very least, make sure you get where you need to go with as little burden on you? Besides, relieving you of this stress will make you clearer of mind so we can get this thing finalized. Sounds like a perfectly valid business expense if you ask me." He leaned over and smiled, his voice cajoling. "Come on, I know you want to say yes. I know you enjoy being able to have unlimited Coke Zero and an ample supply of those peanut butter M&M's you so desperately love."

She looked side-eyed at him. He was more observant than she sometimes gave him credit for. "We'll see."

Only, at five fifty-four, the time her flight to Seattle was scheduled to take off, she was on her fourth soda, waiting for the final word that Ken—their contact at Blossom Brew —had signed on the dotted line while also searching any available flights that would get her where she needed to go by tomorrow morning.

"Are you going to be doing that much longer?" James asked from his position on the leather chair across from her. She followed his gaze to her hand, where she'd been whipping the pencil against the seat of the couch in a frenzied pace. "If I were anything like you, I'd have flown across the room by now and ripped the pencil from your hand," he said, referencing her stealing his tennis ball earlier.

"I don't understand the holdup. What's taking so long?" she asked for the millionth time, ignoring his dig.

James picked up his cell phone and typed another text, one of several he'd been sending and receiving for the past hour. "You know how the Blossom folks are. They're probably waiting for their eight attorneys to read everything backward and forward before translating it into Aramaic and back to English before they officially sign. It might be hours before it's back to us to review. Maybe even tomorrow morning, just cutting shy of our deadline with the bank. They certainly have a flair for the dramatics."

"Unlike others..." she said under her breath and tapped her pencil again as she calculated the time it would take her to get into Eureka if she caught a ten a.m. flight to Seattle.

His phone chirped from another incoming text. "Hmmm," he said, studying it.

"What? Was it from Blossom? The bank?"

"Actually, it's from my pilot. Wanted me to know that he's readied a flight plan that would entail leaving San Francisco tomorrow morning at eight and arriving at 10:12 a.m."—he paused to read from his text—"at a Hartford Airport, fifteen miles outside Eureka, Idaho. From there, arrangement have been made for a private car to take you home." He met her gaze again. "Which would mean that, even if the contract doesn't get signed and returned by tonight, we could still sign and fax it back while en route on our flight."

She flipped the pencil against the desk again, her mind whirling at the possibility of taking him up on his offer.

Hartford was just minutes from Eureka, compared to the hour-long drive she'd be taking from Spokane.

"But what about your trip to Cabo?"

"Still on. I'd just be arriving closer to six tomorrow night."

She bit into her thumbnail, gnawing at it as she considered her options. Catch an early-morning flight to Seattle along with a hundred other passengers before deboarding and waiting another hour for the flight to Spokane, where she'd then have to still drive to Eureka, or...take a private plane.

No layovers. No crowded, germ-ridden cabin. No long, arduous drive through a snowy mountain pass to get home to her parents. A quick two-hour flight and she'd be home.

She closed her eyes. "Fine. Let's do it. But only because you can write this off as a business expense, seeing as how I'm doing *you* a favor—not the other way around."

"Of course. So should I tell Chris to file our flight plan?"

She was weak. So weak. She just had to remind herself that the end result—getting away from the alluring influence of a certain CEO—would be worth it.

"I guess so."

"ALL GOOD?" James asked Quinn the next morning, only half an hour from their destination.

The wilds of northern Idaho.

The place where Quinn Taylor was born and raised. James had to admit to having more than a passing curiosity about the place.

"It's all good," Quinn said. She studied the contract for another moment then handed it back to him to sign.

James was scribbling his first name when the plane

jerked to the right. Quinn gasped and he glanced over to find her gripping her arm rests for dear life.

It wasn't the first time the plane had jumped or jerked from side to side as they headed farther north. Thanks to a winter storm moving across the Pacific Northwest, their turbulence had been steadily increasing. And although James was fairly used to a little flight turbulence, judging by Quinn's pale face, she was still adjusting.

He finished signing the contract that had only arrived half an hour ago—more than sixteen hours past when promised. With this signature, they were in the final stages before the deal would be done. "I think this calls for a celebration." He unbuckled his seat belt and headed over to the minibar, where he pulled out a chilled bottle of champagne.

"You certainly come prepared," she muttered. "You do realize it's barely nine-thirty in the morning."

Uncorking the bottle, he carried it over along with two tumblers. "I thought it would be a nice touch to celebrate both reaching this point in the negotiations, and starting our vacations."

Before she could refuse, he poured them each a glass, pausing as the bubbles reached the top. "To new endeavors."

She clinked her glass against his and took a sip. The plane shifted again, and James barely managed to miss spilling on the newly signed contract.

"Here." Quinn stood up. "I'd better get this faxed off before we have to start all over again."

He picked up his drink and watched Quinn walk a little unsteadily across to the fax machine. His attention, however, was on more than just her careful pace.

It had been a hell of a surprise when his town car pulled up to Quinn's address and she appeared in the doorway wearing a pair of faded blue jeans that fit snugly over long legs and slim hips, a white tee shirt with a wide vee-neck, and a fitted blazer. Nothing fancy but there was something infinitely sexy in its casual simplicity. Something he had never seen on Quinn before and he was still processing how he felt about that.

Then there'd been her eyes. Clear and bright, despite the chilly February morning, made even bigger since, for the first time since he'd met her, she wasn't hiding behind those monstrous glasses. He could finally see the delicate features of her face, the pert nose that turned up the slightest bit at the end, the cheekbones he'd never really noticed, and long, thick lashes that framed those dark eyes to perfection. Her lips, however, he'd certainly noticed those before.

Unaware of his utter shock as he stood there, still halfway out of his town car, Quinn had hopped down the stairs, her low ponytail bouncing jauntily as she dragged her carry-on behind her.

And he'd realized in that singular moment how much he was going to miss seeing her face.

Sure, it was only for a few days, but for some reason he was certain it would feel like longer. Something that even now he was trying not to think about as they drew closer to her destination.

He was relieved now to have somewhere else to be, somewhere where Quinn's absence wouldn't be so noticeable.

"And they're off," Quinn said, watching the pages pull through, a small smile of satisfaction playing on her lips.

The plane dipped suddenly, and Quinn fell forward, catching herself against the wall. James jumped up, helping to steady her as he guided her to a seat.

"You okay?" he asked, studying her face that had gone from pale to a slight greenish hue.

"I don't know. Are we about to die?" She forced a laugh, but the humor didn't extend to her eyes.

Their co-pilot peered his head from the cockpit. "It looks like we're going to be experiencing a rough ride for this last leg, so you two will want to buckle up and sit tight."

Although Quinn's seatbelt was already latched, she pulled at it, tightening it so much he wondered if she could still breathe. The plane rocked again and Quinn placed her head down over her legs.

"It's going to be fine. You just need to relax," he said, trying to instill as much calmness to the situation as he could. "I've been on much rougher flights than this. Why don't you tell me about what you have planned for the next few days in Bazooka?"

"Eureka," she said, sitting up to glare at him. Exactly as he was hoping for—to see a little fight return. "You know what? Let's skip the talking."

"Sure. If that's what you want." James slipped his hand in his pocket and retrieved his trusty tennis ball. Aware of her gaze on him, he threw it against the side of the plane before capturing it. He repeated it, counting down how long it would be before his traveling partner confiscated the ball, maybe earn a little more color in her cheeks as she did.

Only, instead of the sharp reprimand he'd been waiting for, Quinn lurched to her feet and ran in the direction of the restroom.

QUINN GROANED from her perch in the tiny airplane bath-room, holding the wet towel to the back of her neck as she tried to recover her composure. At least she hadn't lost it—not directly in front of him anyhow. And they'd arrived alive and in one piece.

There was a knock on the door. "Quinn? You doing all right?"

She stood up and turned the water on at the sink. "Much better. Just a minute."

The water was soothing as it ran through her fingertips, and she took a moment to dab some around her mouth and face before studying her image. She'd definitely looked better.

From her handbag she pulled out a Tic Tac that she tossed in her mouth before applying a dab of plum-colored lip balm to her lips, something she'd picked up at the Clinique counter a few weeks ago. She scrutinized her appearance again. Still white as a sheet, something that a dab of the balm onto the apples of her cheeks significantly improved.

Knowing it was about as good as she was going to get, Quinn opened the door, spotting James over by the cockpit in conversation with their pilot. From the serious expressions on their faces, she guessed she'd missed something. "Everything okay?"

James glanced over to her and nodded. He patted the pilot on the shoulder and came to meet her. "Just a little bit of a hiccup. That's all."

"Hiccup?"

"The pilot was doing his post-flight inspection and noticed a couple of things that he'd like a maintenance tech to take a look at before we take off."

"How long will that take?"

James ran his hand through his hair. "Not really sure. Fortunately, the FOB—sorry, that's basically the company who operates the private terminal here," he explained. "Anyway, the FOB has a couple of maintenance technicians here on staff, but it's going to be at least an hour before anyone can take a look. From there, it just depends on what they find and what, if anything, it will take to fix it."

"So you're just going to hang out here at the plane then?"

"Don't worry. It will be fine. I'll just watch a movie or maybe take a nap until they have things figured out. Maybe I'll see if you left any of those peanut butter candies to tide me over for lunch."

The guilt hit her. James would be halfway to Cabo if he hadn't gone out of his way to get her this far. And she knew something else he didn't. She'd eaten all the candy.

"Ms. Taylor?" It was their copilot. "Your car is here. I can carry your luggage for you if you'd like."

She couldn't just abandon James. Could she?

"You should go on ahead," James said, nodding. "I know you have lots to do. Don't mind me. I'm sure I can turn up some blankets somewhere to keep me warm." For good measure, he rubbed his arms, although she had to concede that, with the door open, the air inside was gradually growing chillier by the minute.

Okay, so she could see plain as day through his martyr act, but it didn't change the fact that he was here, stranded, without food or a ride for the foreseeable future. She sized James up. What kind of trouble was she inviting if she did what she was considering?

She knew she was going to regret this. "Okay. Just putting this out there, and I completely understand if you would prefer to hang around here, but did you want to tag along with me until you hear something? I'm meeting my sister at the diner for brunch and you could grab something to eat. It's only a fifteen-minute drive away so if you happen to get cleared for takeoff, the car can have you back here in no time."

He scrunched up his face in indecision—as if he hadn't been angling for the invite from the beginning. "Well, I am pretty hungry, and if you don't think I would be in the way or anything." He grinned then, entirely too happy over the sudden state of events. If she hadn't seen the concern on the pilot's face herself, she'd have thought he'd maneuvered the whole thing.

She smiled back, baring a lot more teeth than probably necessary. "No problem at all."

Heaven help her. Quinn wasn't sure what she was more worried about, his impression of her humble hometown, the eccentricity of her family and friends...or her family and friends' impression of him.

He smacked his hands together. "Let's go then. Does this mean I'm going to meet the lovely Sabrina?"

She narrowed her eyes. "Don't even think about it, pal. If you try anything with her, you'll find yourself left on the side of the road in the Coeur D'Alene National Forest."

"I'll try to remember. All set?"

She studied his outfit of cargo shorts, a white short-sleeved linen shirt, and brown leather sandals that probably cost more than the entire monthly rent she and her roommates paid. "I'm guessing that your luggage is probably going to contain more of the same clothes you're wearing?"

"If you mean do I have anything more appropriate for a lumberjack or a mountain man, I'm afraid not. It didn't seem appropriate for the beaches of Cabo."

"Then I guess we should go."

She slid on her black jacket and leather gloves before wrapping the purple cashmere scarf around her neck. With a worried glance James's way, she took the lead to the door and stepped outside.

She stopped short when a cold, biting gust of wind nearly took her breath away. Good thing she still had her winter parka tucked away in a closet at her parents' home. Pulling the jacket tighter around her, she gripped the rail and slowly descended the steps until she was on firm but icy ground.

Three seconds later, a curse streamed from James's mouth, and she glanced over in time to see feet flying out from under him as he reached the bottom step, even as he managed to right himself by grabbing the rail. She bit her lip to stop the laughter bubbling up at the sight of the usually *GQ*-suave playboy fumbling, obviously outside his element.

Maybe this wouldn't be so bad after all.

7

HOLY MOTHER OF—

James clenched his teeth. It felt like he was being sliced in half, the cold was so sudden and biting.

How the hell could anyone function when the wind chill alone had to put the temperature well under zero degrees? It had to be, maybe minus five degrees. He slid into the warmed town car and took a look at the temperature reading.

Huh. Twenty-two degrees. Fahrenheit.

Well, that probably didn't take into account the wind chill, so he might not be off the mark. He sat still, fighting the need to shiver, to chatter his teeth, anything to get the blood moving again. But he wouldn't give Quinn the pleasure of seeing him struggle, especially when she smiled smugly at him and sank back into the seat, far more prepared for the temperature drop than he was. James forced himself to relax, crossing his leg over his knee casually.

While Quinn gave their driver the directions to where they were going, he stared out the window. The sky was gray and gloomy, painting everything in a smudgy charcoal. The surrounding mountain range, however, almost appeared deep blue as it soared around the small valley.

He supposed it was rather beautiful. That is, if he stayed in the well-heated car and avoided the five-foot-high snow banks that lined the sides of the road. He glanced back at the company's Gulfstream sitting on the side of the tarmac waiting to be pulled into the hangar for inspection. It felt like he was saying good-by to the last bastion of luxury and comfort as he pushed forward into the unknown wilderness.

Okay, so maybe he could be a touch melodramatic at times.

The more he considered it, James came to realize he had a lot to look forward to. He'd be able to see the small town where Quinn Taylor grew up, and maybe meet a few of the people who made her who she was. A little more time with the woman before they went their separate ways on vacation wouldn't be too bad, either.

With Quinn seemingly lost in her thoughts, James found the drive surprisingly quiet and peaceful, as he was left to enjoy the view. It wasn't too long before they passed the sign reading *Entering Eureka, Population 7,131*, and he leaned forward to see what it might bring.

It was, quite honestly, breathtaking.

The small town rested not only on the shores of a glimmering lake but at the base of several surrounding snow-capped mountain ranges. All that was needed was an opening in the clouds, as the sunbeams broke through below for it to be picture perfect.

"It's beautiful," he said, and glanced over to Quinn who had been studying him for who knew how long.

He seemed to have said the right thing as Quinn smiled

and nodded before looking back outside. "It is. Every time I come home, I tell myself that same thing. You should see it in the summer, when everything is vibrant and green and the boats are out on the lake."

They arrived on a small street that appeared to be the main artery of the town. The car slowed down to allow people to meander across the street. Most of the storefronts were carefully maintained two-story brick structures that ran along one end of the block to the next. He spotted a local hardware store, a movie theatre, a pizza shop, a coffee shop and bakery, several boutique shops, and even a brewery that made it clear that, although it might be small, the town was lively and burgeoning.

Their driver pulled into an open parking spot in front of a building with a sign above it identifying it as the Eureka Diner. "I texted Sabrina already. She's inside waiting." She grabbed his arm, her tone low and warning. "Remember what I told you."

"Best behavior. Scout's honor."

Again, the cold temperature cut right through his linen shirt, and although the sidewalk was freshly cleared of snow and salted, he still found himself skating across its surface. A gurgle from behind had him glancing back suspiciously. Quinn smiled innocently.

The lingering smell of bacon, maple syrup, and coffee hung in the air as they stepped in, and James looked around, surprised to see the place fairly busy for the mid-morning hour. Immediately, a spry brunette with blue eyes and dark brown hair the same color as Quinn's, hopped up from her seat and ran over, grabbing Quinn in a tight hug.

"You're here, finally! I can't tell you how worried I was that something was going to come up and you wouldn't make it."

"Let's just say I thought a few times we might not make it," Quinn said and stepped back. "First, let me introduce you to James Thornhill, my boss. James, this is my sister, Sabrina."

"A pleasure." He offered his hand to the younger Taylor girl, who was a couple inches shorter and a little curvier than her older sister. She was cute; her easy smile infectious as she shook his hand.

"Nice to finally meet the tyrant whose business seems to take up all of my sister's time these days."

"Guilty. But that should all change now that this deal we've been working on is almost done."

"Maybe, maybe not. Knowing my sister, she'll immerse herself in some new make-or-break project soon enough. She likens herself to some sort of crusader. It's part of an irksome martyr complex she suffers."

"You'll have to forgive my sister," Quinn said, looking exasperated. "She's a writer, so she errs on the side of dramatics, like someone else I know."

They took a seat in the booth, the girls on one side and James alone and left to the intense scrutiny of both Taylor sisters. "A writer, huh? What kind of stuff do you write?"

"Well, right now I'm writing for the *Eureka Examiner*, but I also dabble a little here and there." The sisters shared a grin before Sabrina changed the subject. "Quick status update. The lead guitarist for the three-man band has the flu, and they're trying to find a backup in time for tomorrow night, but it doesn't look promising. They gave us a name of a DJ we might want to call as a precaution. There's also been a delay in the shipment at the florist, leaving a question as to whether we'll be able to have peonies as the centerpiece on the tables. Oh, and Aunt Bea called and left a rambling message apologizing for not being able to make it to the big party."

Quinn gasped. "Did they hear it?"

"Fortunately, I caught that one before Mom could hear it, and I erased it. There've been a few other close calls but I think we're safe. With the winter carnival going on, they've been too busy to notice much of anything. They spent this morning down at the lake watching them put the finishing touches on the floats."

"Floats? As in...parade floats?" James asked, interrupting the flow of conversation.

"It's Eureka's annual winter festival this week," Quinn explained.

A winter carnival. The idea was intriguing. "What exactly happens for this winter carnival?"

"Oh, lots of things," Sabrina said, excited. "Besides the parade of lights, the Eureka ski resort holds some winter events on the slopes, like a race and a torch parade and a laser light show. There's also the food fair and beer-tasting fest at the brew hall tonight, followed by a live music concert at the local dive bar. Tomorrow will be family bingo night, sleigh rides, Mom and Dad's party, of course. Oh, and there'll be the usual exhibition show later this evening from our very own Eureka Roller Derby Girls."

"Roller Derby?" Now he was really intrigued. "They still do that sort of thing?"

"Oh, you'd better believe it. In fact, Quinn here—ouch!"

"You don't need to share all those boring details with James, Sabrina." Quinn's face was suddenly infused with color. "Why don't we go ahead and order so he gets a chance to eat something before his pilot calls—"

"Wait. I have to know. Come on, Sabrina," he said, seeing

the glacial expression Quinn was shooting her sister. "Tell me what you were about to say about Quinn, here."

Her sister smiled unapologetically. "Just that Quinn was Eureka Roller Derby's top jammer three years in a row. She's practically a legend."

Now he couldn't wipe off the grin that stole across his face as he stared at Quinn, who, despite the murderous gleam in her eyes, was flushing. He tried to imagine the practical, no-nonsense Quinn in the full Derby girl uniform, maybe some black fishnet stockings under a pair of tiny bike shorts, bright striped socks or leg warmers over those shapely calves, not an entirely unattractive image. Actually, a quite enticing one.

"Do you think your parents might have some pictures of your sister during her heyday? I don't think I could believe it unless I see it for myself."

This time a booted foot smacked him square in the knee and he winced. Quinn smiled sweetly at him.

"Why, if it isn't Quinn Taylor," said a woman around Quinn's age with short almost-black hair, a nose ring, and wearing a shirt and apron with the moniker of the diner emblazoned across them. "I figured I might see you this weekend, what with the shindig you've got planned for your folks."

The server looked over to him and her mouth went slack.

"Hello," he said. He was nothing if not polite.

"Mandy, this is James Thornhill. We, uh, work together."

The woman's brows shot up. "How...chummy," she said in a tone that made James feel as if he ought to come to Quinn's defense.

"Yes, I'm afraid that while giving Quinn here a lift back home, my plane took a bit of a beating and needs some servicing. But I can assure you, after my lunch, the folks of Eureka will be rid of me and Quinn can enjoy her much-earned vacation."

The woman nodded slightly but she still appeared skeptical.

"I'll have the French toast with a side of bacon and a Coke Zero." This seemed to bring the woman's attention back to the task at hand, and she wrote down their orders and left.

"Great," Quinn said, giving her sister a disgruntled look. "Had you mentioned that Mandy works at the diner, I wouldn't have risked coming here. How long do you think we have?"

"With Mandy? We should probably head out now," Sabrina said and laughed.

"Am I missing something?" James asked. "How long do you have until what?"

"This is a small town, James," Quinn said patiently. "Not a lot happens here, and when it does, the news spreads like wildfire. And we just ran into the biggest gossip of them all." She glanced around. "I don't see her. She's probably on the phone now. Should we try and beat them home, just in case?"

"I'm still at a loss here."

"Mandy no doubt is spreading the alarm that Quinn's not only in town, but she's here with you," Sabrina said, filling him in. "A guy being chauffeured around town in a fancy black car, who shows up in an outfit more appropriate to the Mexican Riviera than Eureka, Idaho, and who also dropped the fact he owns an airplane. That's newsworthy here."

"Well, it doesn't exactly belong *to me*. It's a company plane, you see."

"Yes, I'm sure they'll appreciate that distinction," Quinn said wryly. "Anyhow, the idea was to surprise my parents with my arrival, and the longer we sit here, the more we risk that someone's going to spill the beans I'm back in town—which won't go over well if they hear it first from anyone else."

"It also wouldn't help that our mom's a terrible cook and she takes a certain...umbrage that people might prefer the diner's food to hers."

"Which we do. So should we head out?" Quinn repeated.

"Nah. We might as well enjoy the food while we can. It might be the last decent meal any of us will get today."

Quinn sighed. "I suppose you're right." She leveled an earnest look at them both. "But eat fast."

FORTY-FIVE MINUTES LATER, with no news yet from his pilot, James, Quinn and their driver were heading to Quinn's parents' house with Sabrina leading the way in an old blue Chevy truck.

Near the outskirts of town, they followed a narrow road that turned onto an even narrower snow-covered lane. The Chevy slowed as Sabrina hung a right, then followed a long driveway that led them toward a homey-looking two-story log home with a dark green-pitched roof. It wasn't nearly as enormous or fancy as the two homes James had glimpsed from the road, but it had its own charm. Not to mention that he could see the lake less than half a mile away and well within view.

Quinn was wringing her hands together, something she'd been doing since they left the diner.

"So you're okay with this? Me meeting your parents?"

"Of course. That is, if you're okay with meeting them?" She sounded uncertain, something he wasn't used to hearing from her.

"I look forward to it."

Her sister had already reached the front door by the time they got to the back of the car and pulled out Quinn's luggage. James took a moment to consult with the driver before following them both inside.

"Mom? Dad? I have someone here to see you guys!" Sabrina shouted.

"Someone's here?" The voice was female and coming from the back of the house, the direction where Quinn and Sabrina headed, him on their heels, down a wide hallway that opened into a great room with large cathedral ceilings and two-story windows that faced out onto the lake. "Who on earth would be making their way to see us now?"

A tall, slim woman with the same dark brown hair as her daughters, only worn shorter, appeared, stopping short when she caught sight of Quinn. She squealed before rushing forward to hug her daughter, just as Sabrina had done earlier.

"Bill!" the woman shouted. "Get in here! You won't believe who's here!" Her mom stood back and looked her daughter over. "How I've missed seeing your face." She glanced over to James, her eyes bugging out. "Oh. I didn't realize. And who did you bring with you?"

She said it in such a way as to imply their relationship was something more romantic.

"James, this is my mom, Cindy Taylor. Mom, this is *my boss*, James Thornhill. You remember me telling you about him?"

"All good things, I hope," James said and stepped forward to take her hand. "Nice to meet you, Mrs. Taylor."

"Please, call me Cindy." She took a moment to study Quinn before returning her gaze to him. "Wait. I don't understand. You and your boss are here together?"

"What's this?" an older man somewhere in his mid-sixties bellowed as he stepped into the room. He sported a thick mustache on his upper lip almost as if to make up for the sparse light brown hair on his crown. But it was the suspicion and shrewdness in his light green eyes that glared at James as if demanding to know *who the hell are you* that had James cautious. "You're dating your boss?"

"No," Quinn practically shouted as she flushed scarlet. "James was on his way to his own vacation in Mexico, but when I missed my flight, he offered to get me here on the company jet. He's only here now because he's waiting to hear word from the pilot that they can take off again after we hit some turbulence. Once they've looked over the plane to make sure there wasn't any damage, they'll be taking off again."

"But why's he *here*?" the man repeated, his gaze still on James.

But instead of being intimidated by the man, Quinn shook her head and laughed before hugging him. "I couldn't very well leave him abandoned on the runway. Besides, the better question should be why am I here, should it not?"

Her dad finally pulled his gaze from James and to his daughter, his eyes softening the slightest bit as he returned her hug.

"I thought I'd surprise you both for your anniversary," Quinn said, stepping back. "I hope you don't have anything planned for tomorrow night, because Sabrina and I were hoping to take you two to dinner."

"We're thrilled, absolutely thrilled to have you both here, no matter the circumstances," Quinn's mother said and smiled at James. "And thank you for getting our daughter here safely. James, in case you didn't catch it, this is my husband, Bill, who I'm sure is just as pleased as I am that you're here."

"Nice to meet you, sir." James offered his hand to the surly man, who grunted but accepted the offer.

"I bet you're both starved and I was just preparing lunch," Quinn's mom continued. "Why don't we all have a seat?"

"We ate a little on the plane."

"Then you can at least sit down and join us for a cup of coffee. I'd love to hear more about you, James, and how things are working at your new job, Quinn."

"Hopefully not firing a lot of hardworking employees for the sake of the bottom line," Quinn's father said, piercing him again with that stare.

"Yes, well, we generally prefer to retain our hardworking employees," James said, trying to lighten the mood with humor. But from the glare Quinn's dad was sending him, he had missed his mark.

The table was positioned close to the windows with the best view of the lake, and he was careful to wait until everyone took a seat to take his own, not wanting to usurp anyone's place. "You have a lovely home, Mrs. Taylor."

"Cindy. I insist," she said and returned to the kitchen area to grab a couple of coffee mugs that she brought to the table, along with the carafe of coffee. "Bill built this place for us the first year we were married."

"Well, it's a great home. And you can't beat that view."

Quinn's father ignored the compliment. "I'm sure it's nowhere close to what you're used to, with your fancy planes and probably fancy homes. But it suits us just fine."

"I imagine it does."

"So, James, tell us a little about yourself," Quinn's mother said, joining them at the table. "Where are you from, how's your family?"

Quinn looked embarrassed. "Mom, James doesn't want to have to go through all of that."

"I don't mind," he said. "Well, I was born in Seattle, but after my parents died, I moved to San Francisco to live with my grandfather."

Cindy looked stricken, her hand covering her mouth. "Oh, James. I'm so sorry. I didn't realize. So your grandfather raised you? You two must be close."

James took the coffee she handed him and did a noncommittal shrug, which Cindy must have taken for affirmation, as she continued. "And you grew up in the Bay Area. I always wondered what it must be like living in a big, bustling city like that. The schools must be impressive."

"Mom was a middle school teacher until a couple years ago," Quinn explained. "She takes education very seriously."

"I don't know a lot about the public school system in California, I'm afraid. When I was ten, I went to a boarding school in New Hampshire and later, to Vermont."

"You did?" Quinn asked, her eyes a little wider.

He nodded and took a drink of coffee, barely managing to restrain a grimace from the acrid flavor.

Bill shook his head. "Sounds expensive and unnecessary to me"

"Well, I would bet you had a lot of great adventures," Cindy said, staying positive.

James's cell phone chirped, telling him he had a voice-mail. He pulled it from his pocket. Two missed calls and a voice mail? He hadn't even heard it the notification until now.

Quinn leaned over to see the screen. "Yeah, the cell

service here can be spotty. We usually lose it entirely when we pull off the main road, and then it's iffy once we're at the house. That's why the landline here is your better bet."

Sure enough, a few seconds after trying to place his call, the connection dropped. "Would you mind if I use your phone?"

"Not at all. It's on the wall behind you."

This time, the call went through.

Only, the news that his pilot was telling him wasn't exactly what he'd been expecting.

8

"RIGHT. And you'll call me when you have a better idea?" James asked, glancing over at her. Something in his expression put Quinn immediately on guard.

"Okay, thank you." James hung up the phone and returned to his seat. "Sorry about that. Where were we?"

"What was that all about?" Quinn asked.

"Oh, nothing for you to worry about. Although I might be in need of some assistance in finding a hotel for the night."

"There's a Best Western in town, a couple of bed and breakfasts, and there's the ski resort up the mountain," her dad offered fairly quickly.

Quinn met Sabrina's gaze again, both of them knowing his chance at finding a vacancy at any of those was nil.

"With the winter carnival this week in addition to the usual ski season crowd, I wouldn't hold my breath that you'll find a vacancy anywhere," Sabrina said.

"What happened to the plane? Is it bad?" Quinn persisted.

"They're ordering a part from Spokane, but it won't arrive until the morning."

"Well, if the local places are full, there's bound to be something in Coeur D'Alene," her dad offered again.

"Nonsense." Cindy waved her hand. "That's nearly an hour away. No, James will stay here with us. We have an extra guest room. Of course, the guesthouse around back would have been better—that's where Sabrina has been staying for the past couple of years—but the furnace went out last week, so she's been back in her old room."

"The place might be barely a couple degrees warmer than Antarctica. So lucky me has been reliving my childhood these past nine days in my old room," Sabrina said, smiling tightly.

Quinn was still too stunned to commiserate with her sister.

James Thornhill, her boss, was going to stay here, at her parents' house? Not just under the same roof as her—but with her entire family?

She tried not to appear too horrified, even as she tried to figure out any other solution to the situation. From the expression on her dad's face, he was trying to come up with some alternative as well.

"I couldn't impose on you like that," James said, looking nervously at her dad, not that she could blame him. "I imagine Quinn's idea of a vacation didn't include getting stuck with the boss."

Her mom and sister both stared at her pointedly, waiting. Only they didn't realize that Quinn had personal barriers she'd put up between her and James, necessary barriers to stop herself from giving in to the fantasies that had been stealing into her dreams more and more lately.

And if she was just across the hall from him, sharing dinner with him at her family table, inviting him into her little world up here that she called home, things were going to get really, really difficult.

Still. What choice was there?

She sighed. "Of course you're going to stay here. It's only for the night, right?"

After all, she'd spent months working with the man without doing anything she'd regretted. What could possibly happen in one night?

Now that James was officially their guest, Quinn threw a warning glance to her dad, who was chewing his sandwich almost furiously. It was hard for anyone to miss his reluctance.

Fortunately, Sabrina jumped in. "You're actually in luck, James. It's almost fate that you should get stuck here on the same week as the biggest town party of the year. You'll probably barely be around here at all," she added, casting a wary glance over at their dad.

"I guess if you don't think it will be too much of an imposition..."

Her dad wiped his hands on his napkin and sighed. "You're welcome to stay."

Not exactly a warm invitation, but it would do.

"Thank you, sir, and I promise I won't be any trouble. You'll hardly know I'm here. I believe Sabrina mentioned something about a Roller Derby exhibition game. You did say that was later today, correct?"

Sabrina threw a guilty look at Quinn before nodding. "It is. Five this evening followed by the food thing at the beer hall. All the local restaurants and food vendors will be there with their favorite dishes for everyone to sample. Then we can dance it all off at Crawley's." Sabrina glanced at her watch. "Which means I've got to go hole up in the old childhood bedroom if I'm going to hit my word count for the day."

Her mom came to her feet and started clearing the dishes. "Quinn, why don't you show James his room so he can change into..." Her mom trailed off, her gaze stopping on James's outfit. "Did you say you had some luggage, dear?"

He cleared his throat. "I do, back at the plane. But considering that, aside from this outfit, most of the attire consists of shorts, sandals, and swim trunks, none of which I believe will be appropriate here, there's no urgency in having my driver retrieve it until later tonight. In fact, I will probably have him take me into town now, give me a chance to pick up a few things."

Her mother clucked her tongue. "Don't you worry about buying a thing. It would be a terrible waste for you to spend your money on things you'll probably never wear again, especially when I have some things of Bill's that will work nicely." She looked him over again. "Yes, I think they'll do fine."

"Oh, Cindy, that's sweet. But I wouldn't want to put anyone out."

"Nope, I won't hear any objections. There are plenty of clothes that I've been thinking of donating since, in Bill's retirement, his waistband has done a little expanding. I'll be back in two shakes of a lamb's tail."

James glanced helplessly over to Quinn, but she only smiled sweetly in return, enjoying his discomfort. "You heard her. No problem at all. Why don't I show you your room in the meantime."

Quinn led James down the hallway, stopping briefly to

pick up some fresh sheets from the linen closet before continuing on to the spare bedroom. Right next to her own room.

"Here we are," she said and looked around, noticing how much of her mom's sewing and scrapbooking things had taken over the place in recent years. Bags and fabric swatches covered almost every surface.

James cleared his throat again. "I really appreciate your mom offering me somewhere to stay but are you really okay with it? Because if this makes you uncomfortable, I'm sure I could find somewhere else to stay."

She sighed. Of course it would be infinitely easier if he weren't staying under the same roof, but she also knew that he wouldn't be in this situation if it weren't for her, and she couldn't send him out there to fend for himself. "It's fine. Besides, at this point you'd only offend my mom if you said no. So for the next twenty-four hours, you'll be our guest."

"And what about your dad? I might be mistaken, but I don't think he particularly likes me."

"I don't know how much he dislikes you as much as he dislikes what you represent," she said, moving things off the bed and over to a corner in the room.

"Come again?"

"Up until he retired a couple of years ago, my dad worked at the local coal mine for thirty-five years, twenty of those years as the foreman." She pulled the bedding off one side as James went to the other end to assist her. "In this town, there's always been a kind of odd sentiment, an us, the working class, against the rich mining company. The big bad guys who would prefer to cut a few corners to save the bottom line at the risk of the safety of the men my dad supervised. To him, you represent the big companies, the big businesses always watching out for the bottom line."

He was silent a moment as he picked up the fitted sheet from the bed and opened it, looking a little lost as he stared at it like he hadn't seen one before. "I guess that explains a lot. Not just about him but about you. Is that why you went into labor and employment law? To protect employees from the big, greedy hands of the corporations?"

"Here," she said and took the sheet. "They go on the bottom."

He grabbed one end and they silently worked together to get the sheet on as she considered his question. She couldn't deny it. She'd always been well aware of the social and economic difference between those with the power and the money and those without them. "I know, it sounds a little like David and Goliath, everything in black and white, good and evil, but I wanted to be the voice for those workers who were too afraid to lose their jobs to risk speaking out, even though they knew something wasn't safe, or not right."

There was a lot more to it, of course. But that would mean dredging up personal stuff. Stuff she wasn't prepared to go into with him.

"Do you think of me that way?" James asked tentatively "Like I'm just another Dennis or Paul, more interested in the bottom line than their employees?"

He sounded entirely too invested in the question, and she was growing uncomfortable with the intensity of his blue eyes as they studied her. "I don't always know with you, to be honest," she said, smoothing the sheet down and opening the flat sheet. "At times I see glimpses of this pragmatic guy who wants to run things differently, better, more fairly. Who sees the value of every member of his team. But I also think you struggle with who you want to be and who you think you have to be to run this business successfully."

"Fair enough. All of which makes me more than happy

that, despite your concerns about the big bad corporate demons, you still decided to come and work with me. For that, I'm grateful."

"Grateful?"

He grinned, his whole face lighting up in that way that made it difficult for her to breathe. "For whatever situation you found yourself in that made my offer of employment too tempting to refuse."

Oh, right. Quinn stared at him, trying to return his easy smile. Because the reasons for her desperation, her dire financial straits, were something, even now, that felt like she needed to be ashamed of, to hide. Despite what her therapist told her about how the shame, the fear, and the feelings of loss of control over her life that left her feeling so alone were something she should be proud of *overcoming*. And that being honest with others would prevent her from hitting such a low point again.

Nice sentiment, considering that in the past few months of working at Thornhill, two managers had come to her office to discuss their "concerns" over an employee who had mentioned having to take antidepressants or anti-anxiety medicine. She'd told each manager, of course, that their concerns were baseless and that there was no need to worry merely on the basis of their condition alone, and gave some recommendations for accommodations. But she knew that secretly they all were keeping an eye on those employees, just waiting for a moment where they might go "postal."

It was why, other than her friends and her sister, Quinn didn't talk about her own struggles.

"Okay, here are a few things," her mom said from the doorway, saving Quinn from further discussion on the topic. Her mom dropped the armful of clothing to the bed, along with a pair of worn Timberland boots. She turned around and eyed James up and down, her brow furrowed. "Now the pants might be a little on the short side. But with the boots, I don't think it will be that noticeable." She picked up a giant oversized parka. "Here. Try this on."

James cast another helpless look her way, and Quinn couldn't help but smile as her mom helped him into the green coat. "I bought that for Bill four years ago, and for some reason, he just refused to wear it, but I think it should do nicely for you. I imagine the temperature here is quite a shock from the climes of San Francisco."

"Actually, I'm not really all that cold," he mumbled from somewhere underneath the poufy coat, and Quinn bit her lip to stop from laughing. Definitely a far cry from his usual *GQ*-inspired duds.

"No, I insist," her mom said. "I know that you might not realize it now, but the temperature is going to drop quite a bit later tonight, and I'd feel terrible if you came down with something right before you left on your vacation."

"Well, um, thank you."

"You're quite welcome and you be sure to let me know if there's anything else you need." Happy with her work, her mom patted Quinn on the shoulder before she headed back out, smiling to herself.

James pulled off the coat and placed it on the pile before throwing himself back on the bed, tucking his hands behind his head. "So. What's the plan for the rest of the afternoon? I'm afraid that my cell service is currently at zero bars, and as far as I can tell, there's no Wi-Fi in the place. Which leaves me without access to the outside world. So I might as well tag along with you until the big Derby game."

Oh, Lord. Both James and her in downtown Eureka? The

gossip would be going into overdrive when people saw them together.

But it couldn't be helped. "All right. But there have got to be some ground rules."

He raised his brows and waited.

"First, this is a small town. People talk. And I won't have them gossiping for the next millennium about Quinn Taylor's playboy boss who swept into town seducing the entire female population. So try to keep the flirting to a minimum."

"I didn't realize you think so highly of my prowess that you believe I could seduce every female in the entire town. I'm flattered."

"Don't be." She paused for a moment, trying to keep her train of thought, made more difficult by the fact James looked almost absurd lying there on top of her mom's pink floral bedspread. Absurd and...incredibly sexy.

Stop it, Quinn. Rules. Get back to the rules.

"Second, as nice as it may be to have your own chauffeured car, there's no way you're going to drive around town in that thing. It's just too pretentious."

"And how, pray tell, am I going to get around?"

"I'm not letting you out of my sight, so you'll just have to settle for riding in old Bessie with me. Finally, rule number three. You know the bit, what happens in Vegas stays in Vegas? For the duration of your stay, make that whatever happens in Eureka stays in Eureka. Meaning whatever humiliating thing you might see that in any way involves me, you must promise to never mention it again after you leave tomorrow. Never."

"Really?" he asked, sounding far too interested. "Did you have something in particular in mind?" She gave him her most pointed stare, letting him know she wasn't kidding on this point. "Okay, got it. It's all already forgotten." A sentiment ruined by his grin. "Anything else?"

She bit her lip and considered this. "I reserve the right to amend this agreement at any time, but for the time being, just behave."

"I'll do my best."

9

A LITTLE LATER, Quinn pulled old Bessie into a parking space on Main Street and hopped out. At the sidewalk, she turned and waited for James, who was climbing out more reluctantly.

She wouldn't laugh. Not again. Not after finally convincing him that, in the flannel shirt and the brown Timberland boots, he didn't look like a cross between the Brawny guy and Elmer Fudd. Only...he kind of did. Even if in a sexy but nerdy way.

Not helped by that oversized parka that was probably more appropriate for a Siberian Eskimo, but her mom had insisted that he wear it so James didn't get sick, and he was trying to comply, which was kind of sweet of him.

"Go ahead. Laugh. I can already see it in your eyes that you want to."

She bit her lip and shook her head, not trusting herself to speak without doing just that.

"Well, I think it's safe to lose the coat." James slid out of the parka and tossed it into the cab before shutting the door.

"It will be our secret." She waited for him to join her before heading into the first store.

He reached the door first and held it open for her—which gave her a few seconds to appreciate the rugged way the flannel shirt, rolled up around his forearms, hugged every inch it covered, particularly his broad chest and shoulders that seemed to barely be restrained in the fabric. Or how, even dressed like the Brawny guy, James was still a looker, if the two women who were eying him inside the store were any indication.

"Why, Quinn Taylor, who's your new beau?" asked Maxine—who couldn't be a day under eighty—from behind the counter.

Quinn was beginning to realize that maybe she should have added a large sign around James's neck pronouncing him not her boyfriend to head off the inevitable conjecture and comments. Wasn't Mandy supposed to have spread the news by now she was in town with *a coworker*?

"Beau? No, he's not my beau, he's actually—"

"Quinn and I work together. I'm James, by the way," he said, taking Maxine's hand and then her granddaughter Jessica's, who looked a little moon-eyed as he did, despite the burgeoning belly of her ninth month of pregnancy.

"I heard from Sabrina that there was a problem with the order, and you wanted to run through a couple other options with us?" Quinn asked, trying to bring everyone back on task.

"Oh, yes. For the anniversary party." Maxine grabbed a binder that had been on the counter and flipped through it, stopping at a page. "Same thing happened back when your parents got married, if I recall correctly. Your mom had wanted hydrangeas but we couldn't get them in in time, so it was peonies instead. I'd warned her then that getting married in February, on Valentine's Day no less, was going to cause some problems. But she'd had her heart set."

"Really? Hydrangeas?" Maybe this could still be salvaged. "What are the chances that we might be able to pull those off instead by tomorrow?"

"Well, I'm supposed to be getting a shipment in the morning. Let me call my supplier and see what we can arrange."

With her grandmother in the back making the phone call, Jessica turned her attention to the two of them. "So how's it going in San Francisco? Your sister mentioned you're working for some egocentric playboy who has you working twenty-four seven."

James immediately turned to look at her.

Crap. Crap. Why had Sabrina mentioned this to anyone?

"Oh, really?" she chuckled nervously. "Well, you know how Sabrina is. She tends to embellish everything. It's really not as bad as all that. I am here after all. But tell me, how are *you* doing? When are you due again?"

That seemed to do the trick as Jessica began reciting some of the details about heartburn and morning sickness for the next few minutes. It was a huge relief when Maxine came out to confirm they could make the substitute without problems, and they were on their way.

The sun had forced its way through the clouds and was beating down warmly over them as they stepped outside. "The next stop actually isn't far. Why don't we walk?"

"I'm in no hurry."

She turned her face up to the sun, enjoying the warmth. "You know, that thing back there, about you being an egocentric playboy? It was just Sabrina being colorful."

"Don't worry, I didn't take any offense. There's probably some truth in that statement. I have something of a reputation and I have only myself to blame. As my grandfather would tell you."

She studied him, noting his easy smile as he said this, almost seeming unaffected by the fact his grandfather had a low opinion of him. "You and your grandfather seem to have an interesting relationship."

"Really? Why's that?"

"Well, you don't seem to be under the impression that he thinks much of you when you talk about him."

James stared ahead, his face a mask.

"But I think he must have *some* faith in you, or why would he have given you the reins of this company that he spent his life building?"

"Because he was drugged out of his mind and thought he was going to meet his maker?"

"I'm sure there's more to it than that. I mean, if he thought you were so terrible, he could have suggested—gasp—Dennis."

That seemed to earn a slight grin as he turned his blue eyes her way, but he didn't say more.

"If he hadn't cared, why not let you flit away your summers in Europe with your friends, instead of insisting you come home to learn the business? I believe that he does care, even if he has a hard time expressing it to you."

"You're sweet. Naive, but sweet. Cyrus wanted to remind me how little control I had over my life. To remind me who was the boss. Believe me. There's never been any gleam of pride or love in those eyes when they settle on me."

Her heart ached thinking about this man as an eight-year-old boy, losing his parents and everything he knew before being sent to live with a cold, disapproving grandfather, a man who doesn't appear to have shown James the slightest affection. What would that do to a man, a man who, as Quinn was discovering, was more thoughtful and considerate than he wanted to let on? He cared, even if he pretended not to.

"Your dad, he was Cyrus's only child, is that right?" He nodded. "That couldn't have been easy on him."

"Well, to hear Cyrus tell it, my father was as much a disappointment as I am."

"I can't believe that anyone would be that spiteful. I have to believe that he cared about your father or he wouldn't have been so disappointed. And it couldn't have been easy losing his son, no matter how their relationship was at the time of his death. He might have been afraid to let you in, afraid of hurting again."

"Cyrus Thornhill isn't afraid of anything. Least of all some eight-year-old boy who suddenly became his responsibility."

"Maybe, maybe not. But I still think that he wants the best for you. That even if he won't admit it to you or himself, he wants you to succeed. He wants you to love and care for his business just as he did."

"I already do."

She wanted to put her hand in his and squeeze, to offer him some comfort as she sensed the pain underneath his words. But she had the sense to realize that doing so would be entirely inappropriate. And probably unwanted.

"Where are we supposed to be going again?" James asked, stopping as they'd reached the end of the next block.

She looked around, realizing she'd been so engrossed in their conversation that they'd already passed the shop she'd meant to stop at. "Dang. We passed it."

She whipped around, pulling her phone out to check the time. There was a missed text.

"Sabrina sent a message almost twenty minutes ago.

Says she's found a ride and will meet us at the rink." Quinn noted the time. "We should still hurry, though. You can't miss the opening of your very first bout."

"Good idea, considering I don't think I can feel the tip of my nose anymore."

She glanced at him and noticed the end was fairly bright, and she laughed. "Okay, Rudolph. Let's get you somewhere warm."

For a moment, as they turned, their hands brushed against the other, and even through her leather gloves, the connection was alarming, to say the least. She stuffed her hands in her pockets and kept her gaze ahead.

He was her boss, leaving in the morning for some playtime with undoubtedly far more beautiful and desirable women than her. It was best to remember that.

THE PARKING LOT was completely full when James and Quinn pulled up to the warehouse where tonight's game— no, make that bout—was playing. Stepping outside the truck's warm cab, James was given a painful reminder of just how cold it was when the biting wind practically blew through him, despite the extra layer of flannel and boots. With reluctance, he grabbed the parka from the truck and pulled it on, before following Quinn, who was still biting down her laughter, inside.

"There's Sabrina," Quinn said, pointing over to where her sister was standing and flailing her arms to them from the third row on the bleachers.

"What'd we miss?"

"Still on introductions," Sabrina said.

They peered down at the rink where each player was

doing a turn around the perimeter of the rink as their name was called, before sliding back in formation of the team. Just as he'd expected—okay, hoped—the players wore outrageous outfits that veered from sweet baby doll to hell-raiser depending on each personality.

"Who are we rooting for again?" he asked, leaning into Quinn so he could be heard above the cheering.

"It's an exhibition game, remember? They're all on the same team."

The MC, a heavyset guy with tattoos up and down his arms and a long gray beard, stood in the middle of the rink, building up the crowd's excitement. "And I want to send out a big thanks to you, ladies and gentleman, for coming tonight to support these ladies up here. Now, as you all know, for the past few years, as part of our annual winter fest exhibition game, we invite some of our former all-stars to come out and play for us again and tonight's no exception. Ladies and gentleman, let's give a warm welcome to Margo the-Cannonball-Meyer, and Quinn the Ter-Quinn-a-tor Taylor!"

Ter-Quinn-a-tor?

He stared at Quinn, who was frozen in her seat, her eyes wide. "Is he talking about you?"

She didn't answer, however, instead turning to Sabrina. "Why do I have a feeling you have something to do with this?" When her sister grinned, Quinn's eyes narrowed to slits. "You. Are. Dead. Meat."

"Come on, Quinn. You know once you're out there you're going to love it. I thought you could stand to have some of the old fun you used to have. All your things are in the locker room waiting for you."

"Quinn? Are you out there?" the MC asked, putting his

hand over his eyes to shield them from the lights as he scanned the crowd.

James leaned over, unable to resist. "And just remember... What happens in Eureka, stays in—"

He stopped when he saw the warning in her glare, settling instead for contriteness and he looked down, biting back another smile. Reluctantly, Quinn climbed down the bleachers and spoke briefly to the MC before slipping into the locker rooms. As she and the other former Hellhounder changed, the bout began, and he tried to keep track of the fast moving derby players whipping by, shoving each other as necessary.

"Have you ever watched a bout?" Sabrina asked.

He shook his head, and Sabrina gave him a brief explanation, describing how the jammer's job was to get through the blockers and earn points for her team. The women were ruthless as they knocked into each other, occasionally sending someone to the ground, where they immediately got right back up and joined the rest.

Whatever James had been anticipating, however, hadn't prepared him for the reality when, five minutes later, Quinn reappeared. Like the other girls, her red T-shirt had the word *Hellhounds* emblazoned across the chest, only instead of tucking it into her minuscule black flouncy skirt, she'd tied it at the waist, showing a bit of skin both in the cleavage area and also across her midriff. Her long, toned legs were shown to perfection in the almost thigh-high red socks that even the boxy kneepads couldn't de-sexify. Quite the opposite actually.

And then there was her hair. His usually conservative bun-wearing attorney had it down and in two side pigtails to allow the sturdy black helmet to fit over her head.

Genuine pigtails.

He couldn't take his eyes off of her, especially as she skated forward, smooth and sleek, a sexy little bombshell. She couldn't possibly have any idea the effect she was having on him.

Who was this woman? Especially when, as the whistle blew, the women all crowded together in a formation he was hard-pressed to understand. But Quinn was strong and determined, and it didn't take her long to break through, even knocking a couple women out of her way with her hips before she practically flew around the rink.

"Do you think she'll notice if I record it with my phone?" he asked Sabrina.

"Don't worry. I already have someone taping it."

10

"YOU STILL HAVE IT," Sabrina said as Quinn left the locker room later that night, her Derby gear packed away in a bag over her shoulder.

"No thanks to you," she accused Sabrina, keeping her gaze on the exit ahead instead of the guy who, by the swishing sounds coming from the parka as he moved his arms, was right behind her.

What must he be thinking?

After spending so much time perfecting this image of a polished, hardworking, and no-nonsense attorney, to have put herself in a position that might shed her in a different light, she was nervous.

But James didn't seem similarly embarrassed, despite looking like a giant cream puff. In fact, the glint in those blue eyes was unnerving. "Actually, watching that match got me thinking about the company picnic this summer. Company sponsored roller derby. I can see it, can't you? Paul and Dennis whizzing by on roller skates. Skirts optional, of course."

The image of the two men on skates brought a smile to her face. "Only if you're out there, too."

"I wouldn't have it any other way."

They pushed open the doors and a rush of cold wind mixed with snow hit them in the face. Not a lot, just enough to remind her she was home. She loved it when it was like this.

"Are you sure we didn't take a left and end up in the Arctic?" James asked, his teeth chattering. "At any minute, I expect to see a penguin waddle up to me."

"You are such a city guy," Quinn said, rolling her eyes. "This isn't even that cold yet."

"Yet? Good. Then I have something to look forward to. So what is next on the agenda? And please tell me it involves some place with heat, and maybe a little food."

"You're in luck. Food is exactly what's on the menu. We're heading to the beer hall for the whole Taste of Main Street, remember? Then, if it's not past your bedtime, or you're not too tired and cold," Quinn said, her voice dripping with sarcasm, "we usually hit the local dive bar. It's the best place for any kind of action in Eureka."

"I'll do my best to stay awake."

They reached the truck, and Quinn turned around to find Sabrina watching them both with too much interest in her eyes. "So, James. Have you had the one of a kind experience of driving old Bessie here?"

James looked speechless and Quinn was pretty certain she knew where his mind had gone—exactly as her sister had intended. "She means the truck."

"Oh." He caught his breath again. "No. You do know your sister, right? The woman who has to have everything completely under control?"

"I do not. Besides, it's not like you could have handled her."

"Oh? And why is that?"

"Do you even know how to drive, James? I mean, in the time I've known you, you've been chauffeured everywhere."

"I'll have you know, I'm actually a pretty good driver."

She eyed him skeptically. "Really? All right. Here." She held the keys out to him. "Prove it."

Unperturbed, James took the keys. "Bessie is it? Well, I'm an expert at navigating around stubborn women."

Something in his tone told her he definitely wasn't just talking about cars.

Sabrina opened the door and held her hand out for Quinn to go first. Quinn paused. James was already buckling up, leaving the seat next to him looking all too close.

It was no big deal. She'd sat next to James tons of times before, although never this intimately. But it couldn't be helped since any objection she made over the seating arrangement would draw attention to herself. Like it was nothing, she slid across the seat, all too aware of his heat on the other side of her—not helped by the high stick column on the floor had her legs straddling each side, leaving her left leg pressed close against his.

The interior temperature of the cab shot from icebox to furnace in three seconds.

James turned the key, the truck revving to life, before he grabbed the gear stick resting between her knees.

He grinned. "Sorry." Then he moved the gear into reverse before putting his arm on the seat behind her—another step into her personal space that was making her all sorts of crazy—and looked back as he pulled out.

The light scent of his cologne that hinted of leather and something dark like incense surrounded her, and it was hard not to shiver as his breath practically whispered against her neck. She closed her eyes.

Deep breath in, and out.

What the heck was wrong with her? This was precisely why she'd needed time and space away from James Thornhill. To rid herself of these thoughts and feelings once and for all.

And yet, here she was, entertaining them once again, with even more lurid images running through her mind. The temptation to lean into him was making her crazy. In an attempt at distraction, and to escape the nook he'd created for her against his body, she flipped on the radio.

"James seems to know how to handle old Bessie better than you thought, Quinn," Sabrina said from her other side.

"It's not much different than an old Ford my grandfather bought me one summer, right after I'd tangled my dad's old Porsche around a mailbox."

"The Porsche I can totally see," Quinn said, relieved to hear something so reckless, so like the James she needed him to be for her own sanity. "The Ford truck? Not so much."

"Yes, well, he decided that I had clearly not appreciated the Porsche, and chose the truck as a replacement. It worked out, though, since I was working that summer as a line cook anyhow. Made me fit in a little more, helped people forget who I was. Or who my grandfather was. So where exactly am I going?" he asked as they came to a four-way stop.

"Left."

A few minutes later, they were back on Eureka's Main Street, where James pulled the truck expertly into one of the parking spots that lined the river walkway, and the three of them crossed the street. It wasn't hard to figure out where they were going as half the town was already heading to the beer hall on the corner—one of the few places that could handle the dozens of booths that the town's various restaurants and vendors needed.

Quinn breathed in the sharp night air, taking a second to steal a glance at James. How was it possible that even outside his usual polished surroundings, transplanted here in the near wilds of northern Idaho, he still seemed to just fit? And looked damn fine doing it.

Fortunately, neither James nor Sabrina had an inkling of her thoughts as they stopped at the door to pay the entrance fee. The place was packed as they stepped inside, and the cold night air was forgotten as warm, savory aromas filled the air.

Good Lord. She was going to need a bucket to hold everything she was going to eat. At least James was well aware of her eating habits and she wouldn't have to pretend she ate like a bird. Unless it was Big Bird.

She scanned the room, getting the lay of the place that hadn't changed much in all the time the town had hosted this event. The food booths were all placed around the perimeter of the room with tables and chairs in the middle. At the end of the hall was a stage and podium, where the talent show competition would take place—something she hoped to avoid at all costs as memories of twelve-year-old girls dancing too provocatively came to mind.

"What do you recommend?" James asked them.

Quinn met her sister's gaze. "Everything," they said at the same time.

"Sabrina!" It was Bridget over at the falafel booth.

"I'll catch up with you guys later," Sabrina said and disappeared, leaving her alone with James.

Something that was usually par for the course, the two of them often working alone and late at night over the past few months. But there was something entirely different about being left alone with him now.

There was a new type of synergy between them. Unspoken but undeniable. And she didn't know exactly why. She just knew that the attraction she'd had for him that had been building in the past few weeks had turned from a low flame to a bonfire over the course of the day, making her wish she was anyone other than Quinn Taylor, dignified employment attorney. Someone who didn't take risks with her life, always staying the course, understanding her responsibilities.

How she wished she could be someone else sometimes. Someone who, when James had watched her with that wicked gleam in his eyes back at the Derby, would have marched—or rolled—right over to him and planted a bone-melting kiss on that succulent mouth until he cried for mercy.

Who would have pounced on him back at her parents' house in that moment when they'd been tucking in the sheets on the bed and he'd looked all kinds of crazy sexy despite the scrapbook and sewing crap surrounding them. Someone who, when his leg had pressed against hers in the truck like it had, would have rested her hand on his thigh and whispered a few dirty things in his ear like she was some heroine from one of her sister's books.

Instead, though, Quinn cleared her throat, willing herself to be natural. "We like to start on the end, there. Make our way around. There's no skipping and you have to try everything at least once."

He glanced around the hall, his eyes settling on the plates of food. "You can actually eat that much?"

"You might be surprised."

"It wouldn't be the first time."

He did it again. Grinned and gave her that look. Like she was something…wonderful.

Holy Hannah. Get it together, Quinn.

"Okay. Well, let's get started," she said and led the way, hoping he hadn't noticed the way her face had flushed under his intense gaze.

Just remember, Quinn. He's out of here tomorrow. Partying with any number of beautiful women in Cabo, not giving you or this night a second thought.

Don't do anything you might regret.

JAMES WATCHED Quinn finish the last bite of the bratwurst then drown it all down with half a pint of beer from the town's microbrewery. He had no idea where she was putting everything, considering the fact that, before she'd consumed the brat, she'd also had half of a steak shish-ka-bob, a small rack of baby-back ribs, cheese fries, a fried glob of dough she called a scone (he'd been to London, so he begged to differ), an egg roll, a taquito, and a cup of clam chowder.

She leaned back and put her hand over her amazingly still slim stomach. "Okay. Maybe that last bite was a bad call."

"Yes, since, according to your rules, you still have the falafel and custard stops to go."

She squeezed her eyes shut. "Oh. Don't say falafel."

He bit off a laugh just as an older couple in their fifties stopped by. "Why, hello, Quinn. So good to see you."

It seemed like she knew everyone in the town if the number of people who'd greeted her was any indication.

"Tell me, is there anyone here you don't know?" James

asked when the couple wandered off. He took a drink of a pilsner that was actually quite good.

"It's part of that small-town charm. "It's like living in a fishbowl. For better or worse."

He considered that. "You seem to have survived pretty well. Not that I could imagine the great Quinn Taylor ever doing anything that would warrant censure."

She stared down at her empty glass.

"What's this? Don't tell me that Quinn Taylor was anything less than class valedictorian, president of the debate team, and all-around all-star."

She smiled slightly. "Well, you have most of that correct. But let's just say that having that reputation can also make things harder. Not wanting to let people down, living up to their expectations."

"Yes. I imagine that would have been difficult." He studied the prim attorney who was always doing the right thing, making the right choices, being the golden girl everyone could be proud of. It could be tiring, he supposed. As compared to him, who no one really expected anything from but failure.

Quinn suddenly went still, her gaze on something happening by the front doors. He turned around but didn't see anything out of the ordinary, just more people, including a couple towing three kids.

"Anyone you know?" he asked.

She put her hands to her hair and smoothed it down before tucking it behind her shoulders. "You could say that. Crap. They've seen us."

Now he was insanely curious. "Who's seen us?"

"My ex-boyfriend. Just smile and nod. Pretend that we're having a good time."

"I thought we were having a good time."

"Well, try to have a better time." She smiled a little wildly at him, reaching over to take his pilsner and helping herself since she'd finished hers.

"Quinn? Quinn Taylor, I thought that was you," said the blonde female half of the couple as she reached them, pushing a baby stroller in front of her.

"Shelby, hi. How are you?" Quinn asked through a face-cracking smile.

"I'm six months pregnant, with three little ones under foot, so as good as anyone can expect to be," the blonde said and laughed. "How are you doing? Still trying to save the world out there in California?" There was a definite note of derision as she said this last bit.

"I do what I can. Hi, Dan," she said to the dark-haired guy holding a toddler under one arm. A third kid somewhere around nine was hitting the back of the guy's legs, trying to get his attention.

"Hi, Quinn," he said, managing to ignore the tike. "I heard you were in town." He glanced over at James, telling them with a derisive look that he'd also heard she was in town with James. "I'm Dan and this is my wife Shelby and our three kids. I didn't catch your name," he said and held his free hand out.

"James Thornhill." By the grip on his hand, James guessed the guy was sizing him up.

This wasn't awkward at all.

"How's the insurance business?" Quinn asked.

Insurance. James studied the guy. Slim and with that overly earnest expression on his face like he wanted to please people. Yeah, he totally looked like insurance.

"It's doing great—" Dan started.

"Everyone in town has been talking about the fact the two of you arrived in a private airplane—a Gulfstream, was it?" Shelby asked, not apparently caring that she'd cut off her husband mid-speech. "Fancy. Heck, I haven't even been on any airplane, let alone my own private one. But no surprise. Quinn always knew that nothing in this little old town was going to be good enough. I guess working for some millionaire has its benefits," she added slyly.

The toddler who'd been squirming in his dad's arms started to wallop loudly, demanding to be put down. "Well, we didn't mean to intrude," Dan said. "We'll let you two get back to your dinner. It was good seeing you, Quinn." The guy could barely meet Quinn's eyes and appeared almost relieved to have a reason to leave.

"All right," Shelby said with reluctance. "I'm sure we'll catch up later at your parents' party tomorrow anyhow. Mom's fit to be tied with trying to keep this secret from your mom. They never were very good at keeping secrets from each other."

Quinn nodded, her smile still pinned painfully in place. "I look forward to it."

Sure she did.

"That was interesting," James said after they departed. "Shelby certainly seemed to have a lot to say. Something tells me there was some history there that I don't know."

Quinn shrugged. "She used to be my best friend."

"Wait. Your best friend married your ex-boyfriend? How did that happen?"

"Shelby made the unilateral decision that friends should share everything when she and Dan slipped away to the boy's locker room. During our senior prom. If that wasn't hard enough, little Sawyer came along nine months later."

"Ouch." He didn't know much more to say.

She studied her empty plate. "You know, I think I could use some fresh air. Want to take a walk?"

"Sure." He grabbed their plates and dropped them in a large garbage bin and followed her out. "What about Sabrina?"

"Oh, we'll catch her at Crawley's. It's just down the block."

For once, he was grateful for the poufy warmth of the parka as he pulled it around him, the high top of the lumberjack boots that kept his feet dry and steady. He glanced at Quinn to see how she was doing, but if she was cold, she covered it well as she took long strides on the sidewalk, her face tucked into the light purple scarf wrapped around her neck.

He waited until they'd crossed the street and were on a path that led around the lake to say anything. "I'm sorry."

That caught her attention. She looked over at him. "For what?"

"Sorry that the two people you thought you could trust would do that to you. I can't imagine how that must have hurt."

"Oh. I was over that a long time ago. Really. I made no secret of the fact that I was going to leave Eureka and go away to college. I knew that Dan was sticking around. We were on borrowed time anyway."

"Yes, maybe. But every minute of that time with you should have been cherished and appreciated. Not wasted on someone like Shelby." Because as much as Quinn was "fine" now, back in high school, when everything was more dramatic and scrutinized, having your best friend boyfriend hooking up behind your back could not have been easy. "You're way too good for him. For both of them."

She seemed surprised at his comment before her lips twisted into a smile. "Thank you." She considered something for a minute, and he waited, the grinding sound of their feet over salted concrete filling the air. "I guess I also shouldn't have been too surprised. I mean, back then, when Shelby and I walked into the room, it was usually Shelby who drew people's attention with her open, assertive manner. She was the fun one, while I was more cautious. Reserved. I suppose I should be relieved that Dan didn't throw it all away on some one-night stand. That they actually are a better fit than I ever envisioned."

"If you mean a better fit in that they're two of the phoniest people I've met—and that says a lot, for me—then I suppose you're right."

"I don't know. Maybe." She kept walking, quiet again.

It bothered him that some faithless ass-hat like Dan had been able to hurt someone as strong and resilient and loyal as Quinn. It made him wonder if that guy was to blame for Quinn's lack of a love life—or any interest in having a love life.

"I mean it," he repeated. "You could do better than Dan. You have a lot to offer someone, Quinn. Any guy would be lucky to have your love."

She laughed. "Things must have looked worse than I thought if I'm getting a pep talk from you."

He grinned. They continued on the sidewalk that ran parallel to the lake where a thick, low-laying mist made it impossible to see the frozen water's surface.

"What about you?" she asked. "Sure, you've dated a lot of women—and I use the word 'women' loosely since I'm sure a couple of them were barely legal—but has there ever been anyone you've been serious about? Who you thought just might be the one?"

"The one? As in, anyone I could see spending the rest of my life with?" He pretended to consider that. "I'm afraid not.

Why have one when the whole world is out there for the taking?"

She rolled her eyes. "I'm serious, James. There's never been anyone?"

"I'm afraid that finding someone, putting down roots, is something that would only please my grandfather. And that's the last thing I'd ever want to do."

"So you don't ever want to get married, maybe have a family?"

He shrugged. "To tell you the truth, the thought of just one person, the whole now-and-forever thing, has had zero appeal for me." Not to mention giving any one that kind of power over his emotions, over his heart, wasn't anything he'd risk. Not again.

"Don't tell me you're one of those jaded self-important people who thinks there's no such thing as love and marriage and happily ever after."

"Not at all. I'm a big believer that there can be forever and happily ever after for the right people. I just have never been one of those people. I've always liked my freedom, my independence."

Although, if he were being honest, that tight insistence on maintaining that indifference, that independence, had been getting harder of late. Feeling less a choice and more a curse. Especially since the day that Quinn Taylor walked into his life. Filling his once solitary almost boring days with something altogether more exciting and enticing.

"Love and commitment are not exactly a death sentence," she said, laughing at him.

Time to turn the spotlight to someone else, since he wasn't ready to analyze his conflicting emotions. "So are you saying that you want that for yourself? Love? Commitment?

Because if you do, you might actually have to go out on a date every once in a while."

"I've dated."

"Yes, Chuck, as we've well established. And Dan, and I imagine a few other boring guys in between there. But how about someone who, when you're around him, makes your hands sweat and your heart race and any coherent thought flies out the window? Who smiles at you and your whole world seems to tilt and you're left trying to catch your bearing? Who you can't wait to wake up to because you know that having them in your life had just made everything better."

Whoa. Where had that come from?

As if echoing his thoughts, Quinn stared at him with a funny expression. Then just as quickly looked away. "You know, I'm already feeling better. Why don't we head over to Crawley's? I could certainly use a drink or two. You game?"

"I'm game for anything." And a few drinks that would help him forget the ridiculous comments he'd just made.

And the woman he'd been thinking about with every word that he'd recited.

11

An hour later, Crawley's was near capacity as every available seat in the house was occupied. Fortunately, she and James had arrived early enough to secure seats for themselves as well as Sabrina and her two friends, Bridget and Lindsey.

Something she had questioned the wisdom of when, shortly after the first round arrived, Sabrina decided that a game of "Never have I ever" was a good way to start off the night. Quinn had to admit, now that she'd warmed up, the game was actually a lot of fun. In fact, as prudish as Quinn had thought herself, she'd managed to have already consumed enough beer—and a shot of tequila—to have her convinced everything was absolutely hilarious.

Their waitress set two more pitchers of beer on the table and smiled that come-hither smile James's way before leaving.

Okay. Maybe not *everything* was hilarious.

"All right," Bridget said when everyone's drinks were refilled. "My turn. Let's see." She held her glass up. "Never have I ever gone to law school."

Damn. Another one for her.

Quinn grabbed her full glass and took a drink, relieved that the strong brew that had once wrinkled her nose with the flavor was going down a lot easier by her third glass.

From the corner of her eye, she caught James smiling as he shook his head at her sister and friends, who were barely restraining their glee. Only then did the truth finally dawn on her.

"Have you guys been playing with me the entire time?" she asked, now remembering all the previous proclamations of never doing things like being class valedictorian, maintaining a 4.0 GPA in high school, and riding in a private plane, all of which Quinn had obviously admitted to doing. To her credit, if she recalled correctly, it was only the last couple of declarations that were—now—so transparent.

This time the laughter erupted. "Man, you were too easy," Sabrina said.

"Cheap play. And you couldn't have warned me?" she asked James, who was lounging comfortably in his chair, the red flannel shirt her mom had found for him opened up three buttons to reveal his white tee-shirt and a hint of tanned skin.

He grinned, something entirely too dangerously appealing. "I was trying to see how long it would take you to catch on."

Somehow he made lumberjack sexy.

Or was it the beer? Damn. He couldn't look at her like that, especially when her defenses were down.

"That's it. My turn." Payback time. Quinn cleared her throat before turning toward her sister. "Never have I ever flirted with a cop to get out of a ticket."

She didn't add that she'd never actually been pulled over by a cop...maybe she'd save that one for later.

Quinn looked around the table, satisfied to see every last one of them having to take a drink—James, too. He'd kept up with them, drink for drink, but he didn't seem half as affected. She shook her head. Figures. Nothing could take the polish off this Adonis.

"Okay. I'm up." James drummed his fingers on the table as he studied each of them. His lips turned up into a wide smile. "Never have I ever fallen in love at first sight."

Had she ever fallen in love at first sight? She smiled back at him, not even reaching for her glass.

The rest of the women all took a drink, Sabrina included, who wiped her mouth before studying the two of them with a faintly alarming gleam in her eyes. Fortunately, it wasn't her sister's turn; it was Lindsey's, who was now pointedly staring at Bridget. "Never have I ever read my boyfriend's texts."

"Fine," Bridget said, not appearing the least contrite as she took a drink. "But let me say, it was certainly worth discovering what a two-timing jerk he was."

That's right. Bridget almost married her two-timing jerk.

Although Quinn had never gotten as close to being engaged to Dan, contrary to her assertions to James that she'd always known breaking up with her high school sweetheart was inevitable, she'd actually hoped on some level that maybe, somehow, things would work out. Quinn only wished she'd seen the truth of Dan's infidelity by reading some texts. No, she'd gotten the truth up close and personal when she actually walked in on the two of them that night in the locker room. It was an image of pink and taffeta that was impossible for Quinn to ever forget.

"Yeah. Men suck," she said, commiserating.

"I'll try not to take offense," James said.

She waved her hand. "You know what I mean."

"Okay, Sabrina, you're up," Lindsey said.

"Let me think a moment here." There was an all-too-mischievous gleam in Sabrina's eyes as she stared at Quinn. Sabrina, under any circumstance, liked to stir up trouble—especially when it came to her sister, who she thought needed to relax more and have some fun. Sabrina on alcohol took that mischief level up by a hundred.

Maybe this wasn't such a good idea, coming here with her tonight. But it was too late now, as Sabrina grinned like the Cheshire cat. "Never have I ever wanted to kiss my boss."

Quinn's stomach bottomed out.

Oh, dear Lord. She didn't. She really hadn't just gone there.

Lindsey and Bridget both grabbed their drinks and threw them back, no surprise.

Quinn had to think fast. Sabrina couldn't possibly know the salacious thoughts that had been running through Quinn's mind about James and what it would be like to kiss his perfectly shaped lips. She did know, however, that Quinn had suffered a terrible crush on her night manager at the TGI Friday's where she'd worked her first year of college, which was probably why she'd used that particular question. Quinn's face was growing warmer as she felt every set of eyes at the table on her.

Damn her sister. She was going to totally have to get back at her for this one.

Quinn reached out and grabbed her beer, draining her glass. She needed the cool liquid to help decrease the temperature flooding her face. She set the glass down, finally prepared to meet James's gaze. His right eyebrow was cocked, and he was looking at her with the widest, most arrogant smile she'd ever laid eyes on.

"Tell me. Was he—or she—anyone I know?" From his tone, there was no denying that James believed he was the boss in question.

Rightfully so.

Not that she'd admit that so blatantly. Her head was swimming, and the delicious effects of her tipsiness made her suddenly bold—or stupid. Instead of correcting him, she shrugged and smiled slyly. "Wouldn't you like to know?"

Sabrina and the girls chortled while James nodded, as if to say *touché*. Quinn tried to ignore the flips her stomach was doing.

Where the heck had that come from? This flirty little banter?

Wait. She was overthinking this, something that another glass of beer would help resolve. Then Bridget was up again. "I have the best one. Okay, never have I ever danced with a millionaire."

No surprise, James was the only one taking a drink.

"No way," Bridget said, standing up a little unsteadily, throwing her red hair over a shoulder. "We are rectifying this right now. Come on, James."

James, however, was still watching Quinn, almost expectantly. It took her a moment to realize he was waiting to get her okay.

"Go," she said and laughed.

Besides, it would be good to have a break from the game to catch her breath and have another drink. She ground her teeth together, surprised at how numb they felt. Did they always feel like this?

"No way, we're all going to take this one. Come on," Sabrina said, pulling on her arm. "Up, Quinn."

And whether it was the alcohol that had weakened her

usual inhibitions or the strange heady feeling she was experiencing in James's company, or both, Quinn came to her feet and joined the four on the dance floor.

ANOTHER COUPLE of hours and pitchers of beer later, James made the authoritative decision to call it a night. Especially after, for the third time, he had to step in between Quinn and some half-wit who was trying to get a little too hands-on on the dance floor with his surprisingly sexy little attorney. It was a line dance, for crying out loud.

After slowly driving behind Bridget and Lindsey, who made it to Bridget's brother's place just two blocks away, James drove Quinn and Sabrina home. The two women giggled as they remembered some of the night's highlights, the sound of their laughter bringing a smile to his lips. James had had fun tonight, more fun that he'd have thought hanging around with four beautiful women whom he was prohibited from flirting with. Quinn had enjoyed herself, too, even if she was going to be paying for it dearly in the morning.

"That one just might make it into my next story," Sabrina said, wiping a tear from her eye after the last pitch of giggles died down.

"Into your newspaper stories?" he asked.

This earned another round of giggles.

"You gotta let me tell him, Sabrina," Quinn said.

"Tell me what?"

"I guess he's earned the truth. Let's just say that writing small-town stories for a small-town newspaper doesn't exactly pay the bills," Sabrina began.

"No, remember? The newspaper writing was just a cover for your real job, something I think it's time to come clean about. There's nothing to be ashamed of."

"You're one to talk, seeing as how you still haven't told Mom and Dad the truth about—"

Whatever she was going to say was stopped by Quinn's elbow in her gut followed by Quinn practically shouting, "Sabrina writes dirty romance novels."

James was well aware of the fact that Quinn had cut her sister off before she could make some big revelation that Quinn wasn't ready to share, but he decided to ignore that fact for now. "You're a novelist, huh? Have you—"

"Before you ask, we're not talking about my research techniques."

"Fair enough. But I was only going to ask if your parents were aware that you're a fiction writer?"

"Not. A. Chance."

All too soon, they were pulling in the driveway, and the sisters pounced out of the truck and raced for the door like they were teenagers, slipping in the snow as they went. He dodged a snowball as he unlocked the door before the girls ran into each other trying to be the first in the house, and the giggling started all over again.

"Shh, you guys might want to keep it down," he said, not wanting a confrontation with Quinn's dad, who would probably not take too nicely to James's bringing home both his daughters completely plastered.

"Their room is upstairs," Sabrina said, waving her hand in dismissal. "Once Dad's out, he's out for the count. And thanks to the earplugs Mom wears to tune out Dad's bear-like snores, she can't hear anything. We could hold a rave down here and they wouldn't hear a thing."

"And you should know," Quinn quipped.

They made their way to their bedroom doors, Sabrina turning in first. "Night, you two. Don't do anything that I wouldn't do," she intoned before slipping into her room, her laughter muffled behind the closing door.

Quinn stumbled down the dark hallway, tripping on something unseen on the floor and falling forward. But he was ready and he caught her before she crashed into the wall. He kept his hand around her waist to keep her steady —or so he told himself.

With his free hand, he flipped on the light in her room, taking a moment to look around. Unlike the craft/guest room he was staying in, Quinn's was tidy and minimalistic with a picture or two on the walls and a few items displayed on the dresser and desk. Pictures that he would have liked more time to scrutinize under different circumstances.

"I had a lot of fun tonight," she said. "Did you have fun, James? Did you enjoy yourself?" she said and walked over to her bed and dropped back on it.

"Immensely. It's a night I won't soon forget." Of that he was certain.

"I think it's fair to say that this event fits number two in our rules." She kicked off one of her boots, and then the other. "That whole what happens in Eureka stays in Eureka? You can never talk about this night. Ever."

"Ever? Well, in that case, maybe you'll answer a question for me before I push all the memories from my head. Such as..."

He stopped. What was he doing? He had been about to ask her if she'd been talking about him when she took that drink tonight. When she'd admitted to having thoughts about kissing her boss. That would have been a mistake for so many reasons.

First, unlike Quinn, he was sober and had no excuse for crossing that line, a line that—depending on her answer—would have made things harder to walk back from. Second, he was her boss, the CEO of the place where she worked, and there were just some lines he could never cross. No matter how much he wanted to. He valued Quinn too much as both an employee and a...well, whatever she was that he wasn't going to analyze right now, and the thought of doing something rash that could cost him having Quinn in his life was unthinkable.

"Never mind," he said quickly.

"Oh, I know what you want to know," she continued, tugging off a pair of heart-covered knee-high socks that she had to hike up the leg of her jeans to peel off. "If I'm really as okay about Dan and Shelby as I seem after that little comment I threw out at the bar," she said, clearly *not* knowing. "But I am. I am totally A-Okay with the whole thing now. Really. I mean, I know I'm never going to be as open and expressive like Shelby or Anna and all the other fun girls out there. I'm standoffish. Cold. Boring. And I'm fine with that. People just have to work a little harder to crack this nut."

He laughed, unable to stop himself, as what she'd said was completely ludicrous. She was anything but boring or cold or... "A nut? You liken yourself to a nut?"

She got caught up for a moment pulling the scarf from her neck. "You know, all hard on the outside, almost unbreakable, but once you make the effort to crack me open, I'm soft and complicated on the inside."

There were too many double entendres to that one, and he had to bite back another laugh. "You know, Quinn, just because you're not an open book does not make you cold or standoffish. It's your complexity, your spirit, your drive and determination that have had me enthralled with you from the first moment I met you."

She looked up, smiling like she didn't believe him. "Right. You mean when you had that blonde's tongue down your throat in line at the coffee cart."

He smiled. "Okay, maybe not just then. But sitting across from you at that table a few minutes later, I could see not just intelligence but also passion. Now, why don't you try to lie down and get some rest. You have a long day ahead of you."

She had pulled one arm out of her jacket and was trying to shrug it off but she hadn't unzipped it fully. He kneeled down.

"Here," he said, pulling the zipper free and helping her pull her other arm from its sleeve. He set it on the chair behind him, and picked up the scarf that she'd left on the bed. This, for some reason, he held on to, tucking it into his pocket while she slid back on the bed, her head barely missing the corner of her nightstand.

She stared up at him with the goofiest expression on her face, her eyes nearly closed. "You know, someday you're going to make some lucky girl really happy. Really, really happy."

And just like that, she closed her eyes and, with one last big sigh, was out.

He stood there, looking down at her as she slept. So vulnerable and honest and all too wonderful. He took a moment to brush a strand of hair from her face before stepping back until he was at the threshold of her room.

"Night," he said softly, then turned the light out and shut the door.

Back in his own tiny space, he stripped off the borrowed

clothes and slipped on the pair of (what else?) flannel pajama pants that Quinn's mom must have left for him. Grabbing his cell phone and Quinn's scarf, he sank onto the bed.

He inhaled the soft, familiar scent that still lingered on the scarf, knowing as he did so he was being practically as perv-y as the guys on the dance floor tonight. He wrapped it around his hand and turned his attention to his cell phone to see if it had been updated during his foray into town.

He was surprised to find that he'd received a dozen emails, phone calls, and text messages—and he hadn't checked them even once. Then again, why would he when nothing that anyone could say would be as interesting as what was happening around him?

But now, with nothing else to do but give in to his drowsiness, he decided to see what was awaiting him.

There was a message from his pilot telling him that the part was delayed in Spokane and wasn't expected to arrive until late afternoon tomorrow. Instead of disappointment that his trip to Cabo might be delayed further, however, James felt relief, maybe even a little excited at the prospect of another day in the company of a woman who never ceased to surprise him. He just hoped that Quinn and her family would be as accepting of this change in plans.

He scrolled down further, stopping at one from the underwriter at Crestwood Bank. They needed him to call back to answer some questions that had recently come up.

Well, there wasn't anything he could do about it now, not after midnight. He might as well try to get as much sleep as he could before trying to get to the bottom of this in the morning. He'd borrow Bessie and head into town, where he could get some decent Wi-Fi, cell service, and privacy.

A chance to get away from the magnetism of a certain brunette's smile, to catch his breath, and figure out how he was going to make sure not to let himself fall.

Because falling for Quinn was something he couldn't allow.

12

Her mouth tasted like a skunk had died in it.

Ouch. The sharp stabbing pain in her head wasn't any better.

How much beer had she had last night? Oh Lord. She hadn't done anything too embarrassing, had she? In front of James?

She searched her hazy memories, despite the pain it took for her to concentrate, knowing that there was something there. They'd played the game, done some dancing...

What was it? Oh, right. She'd practically admitted to her boss that she'd been thinking about kissing him while playing that stupid game.

Quinn brought her arm over her face, trying to block the memory. Too late. And had she really flirted with him like that? All she could do was pray that he understood she was only kidding.

Rolling to her side, her stomach instantly churned in protest. But she'd already emptied it hours ago, having barely made it to the toilet in the dead of night before she pulled herself off the floor, took out her contacts, and kicked off her jeans and got back into bed.

Another memory was niggling at her. She'd been lying in bed, her eyes growing heavy and she'd said... What was it? Instantly, she remembered. She'd actually told James that he was going to make some lucky girl really happy one day. *Really, really happy.*

What. A. Bonehead.

There was a knock at her door and she froze in horror. What if it was James? What was she going to say to him after last night? How could she face him—especially if she looked half as bad as she felt?

She bolted up, moaning against the sudden movement before grabbing her glasses from the nightstand where she'd left them when unpacking yesterday. But she didn't have anything to worry about as the door swung open and her sister stood there, looking tired but at least human, unlike Quinn. Sabrina's hair was damp, and her face was flushed, leaving Quinn with a sinking suspicion that her sister had probably used all the hot water for the next half hour at least. Great.

"You decent?" Sabrina asked already shutting the door behind her. She carried in a mug of coffee and a pack of saltine crackers that she sat on the nightstand before taking a seat on Quinn's bed. Taking a cracker from the package, she handed the rest to Quinn, who sat up and tentatively bit into one.

The dry saltiness of the crackers was just what she needed to calm her stomach, a relief considering how much she had to do today. She reached for the coffee. "Okay, so on a scale of one to ten, how much would you say I humiliated myself last night in front of James?"

Her sister chuckled. "You were fine. It wasn't that bad."

"Not *that* bad? That doesn't exactly make me feel any better." She hesitated. "How's he doing? Have you seen him?"

"James? Oh, he left before I was up. Mom said he was planning on finding a place with Wi-Fi and decent cell service so he could take care of a few things."

James was already gone? A sense of sadness and disappointment gripped her. "Do you know if he was coming back?" He could be already heading to the airport again and off to Cabo without so much as a good-bye.

Her sister grinned. "I believe that was the impression Mom had. Hey, do you like this guy?"

"James? Don't be ridiculous. He's my boss." She took a sip of the hot brew before setting it down on her nightstand, careful to keep her gaze diverted.

"Yeah, he is. But that doesn't mean you can't like him. You do like him, don't you?"

Quinn sank back into the pillow. "It doesn't matter if I do or don't. A relationship with my boss is out of the question —that is, if I want to keep my job. A job that is this close to paying off the last of mom's medical bills."

Sabrina was silent, her fingers tracing a pattern on the top of the quilt covering the bed. "I'm sorry that you had to take all that on yourself. But I don't want you to feel you have to stay

tied to a place just because it pays all that money. Especially now that my books are really taking off, I'm sure I can help you out more than before."

"You're helping out enough as it is. I know moving back home, wanting to keep an eye out on mom and be an extra source of support, has helped her more than she knows, or I can repay. And she's happy, really happy, so I'd say that this arrangement of ours has been a success."

"It's true," Sabrina said, smiling again. "I might even broach the subject of moving out by this summer. In fact, when I think of all the loving attention I've been forced to endure by the parental units over the past couple of years, maybe you owe me."

"Don't push it. And don't worry about me, or my job. It hasn't been all bad. Which is why," she said, returning to the point of the conversation, "it's important that I keep that line drawn between James and me. If some of the people at work thought that there was anything more between us, any credibility and respect I've earned would go right out the window. I'd become a punch line. Then we're both forgetting another important fact. Whether I like James or not doesn't mean that he likes me—at least not that way. Having seen the women he likes, I think I'm safe."

Sabrina scrunched up her face. "Don't sell yourself short. Quinn Taylor, you are the real deal, the whole package, and James or anyone would be lucky to have *you*. You're smart and beautiful, loving and kind and generous. Not to mention that you have the most amazing sister anyone could ever ask for."

"Oh, sure, if you mean a sister who likes to put you in really uncomfortable situations. Such as getting me to admit I've ever thought about wanting to kiss my boss. You knew I used to like my night manager at Friday's. And now James probably thinks I was talking about him."

Sabrina grinned unapologetically. "Don't worry about it. It's not like you actually said it was him. It just adds a little more mystery."

"Girls?" their mom called. "I have breakfast ready."

Oh, dear Lord. Quinn was just getting her stomach settled. How was she going to handle her mom's breakfast?

"I'd eat a few more crackers if I were you," Sabrina said

and took two more before getting off the bed. "And Quinn? One last thing. Try not to overthink this. I am sure that everything is going to work out as it should."

With that, Sabrina headed out, leaving Quinn already working overtime to figure out what everything meant—in opposition to her sister's direction.

Including wondering what James was thinking—about her and everything—at that very moment.

JAMES STEPPED out of the truck and came around to the other side to grab the gifts he'd bought from town, including two dozen doughnuts of assorted varieties that were sure to appeal to a wide array of taste buds. Particularly the two custard-filled chocolate-glazed Bismarcks that he knew were Quinn's favorite.

Walking up the snow-covered path to the front door, James smiled as he had every time he thought about last night.

Quinn had been lovely and funny, not to mention sexy and enchanting. He just hoped that he could get this latest snag on the franchise deal settled before he had to worry her. He owed it to her to have a little relaxation and quality time with her family without any distractions.

He knocked when he got to the front door, unsure of the etiquette of entering someone's private residence when he was an invited guest. Quinn's mom appeared a minute later. "James. You don't have to knock, hon. Come on in."

It was hard to miss the pungent smell of burnt bacon as he stepped inside. "Thank you, Cindy. And these are for you." He brandished a bouquet of flowers. "I understand today's your thirtieth wedding anniversary."

She appeared taken aback for a moment, then her eyes swam with tears as she took them. "Why, if that's not the sweetest thing. Thank you."

Before he could prepare himself, she grabbed him and squeezed him in a hug then turned around and, brandishing her flowers in front of her, returned to the kitchen. Still thrown off by the affection, he wiped his feet on the rug and followed.

"Quinn should be out in a minute. She just finished her shower. I'm afraid we already ate breakfast, but I could fix you up a plate if you're hungry."

"No, but thank you. I ate something at the coffee shop in town." Something he'd made sure to do after the warnings of the woman's daughters. "In fact, I had hoped to save you from having to go out of your way to make breakfast by picking up some doughnuts for everyone."

"You didn't have to do that. Well, I'm sure that we'll manage to eat a few so they won't go to waste. I hope you got everything arranged that you needed to in town. And was there any word about your plane?"

"Actually…" he started. But at that moment, Quinn entered the room in a soft cream-colored sweater and another pair of curve-hugging jeans, looking so fresh and beautiful that it was all he could do not to stand there grinning like a star-struck teen. The only sign of her overindulgence the night before was a wince when the bright sunlight streaming in from the lakefront windows hit her face, and she squinted her eyes against the intrusion.

"Quinn, good morning." Scenes from the night before ran once again through his mind. Particularly the way she'd glanced up at him so wistful and sweet as she told him he was going to make some girl really happy.

No, as she'd put it, really, really happy.

She blushed, barely able to meet his gaze. "Morning."

"I hope that shower refreshed you," her mom said, unaware of any undercurrents between them. "Oh, and James brought us some doughnuts, although I'm not sure if you'll want one since I know how sick you were at breakfast—"

She practically lunged for them. "No, I think I've got my appetite back. A little," she added hastily before changing the subject. "I caught the tail end of your conversation. Something about your plane?"

"Bad news, I'm afraid. The delivery of that part has been delayed until later this afternoon, so there's a possibility I might not get out today. My pilot assures me we'll definitely have wheels up by tomorrow morning, at the latest."

"What's that?" Quinn's dad asked lumbering in. "You can't get your plane up?"

James hoped that wasn't a guarded reference to anything other than his plane. "I'm afraid so."

"That's quite all right," Quinn's mother said, ignoring her husband's grunt of dismay. "James, you're more than welcome to stay here. It's not a bother to us at all. In fact, just see what James was sweet enough to bring me this morning." She held her bouquet up. "Wasn't that thoughtful of him? He'd heard it was our anniversary and wanted to do something nice. I don't know when's the last time anyone ever sent me flowers. They're just beautiful."

From the glower James was receiving, Quinn's father wasn't as excited about the gift.

"Look, Dad," Quinn said, opening the box. "James also brought doughnuts for everyone." She held up a thick bear claw that James had been hoping to snag for himself. "Here. Your favorite."

"Actually, I was kind of saving that one for m—" James started.

The old man stepped forward and took it. "Great," he said and sank his teeth into the doughy softness as he met James's gaze and smiled. "Thanks. Well, I'm going to head to the lake. Get a little fishing in."

"Fishing?" James asked, still chilled to the bone from the frigid temperature outside. "As in ice fishing?"

Mr. Taylor stared at him like he was a simpleton. "What else kind of fishing would you think when the lake's froze over?"

"Sorry, it just surprised me. I'm familiar with the sport, of course, but I don't think I've ever met anyone who actually ice fished."

"I have a wonderful idea," Quinn's mom said, clasping her hands together. "Why don't you take James along with you? He has the whole day to kill, and I bet he'd just love to see what the draw is to the sport."

"Actually, there was a matter—a business matter that I needed to discuss with—"

"Hope you don't have any business you want to talk about with my daughter, seeing as how she's here on vacation and off the clock?" Quinn's dad asked accusingly.

James felt a moment of panic and swept his gaze toward Quinn in the hopes of some sort of rescue. A fisherman he was not in the best landscape. But in this temperature? He suppressed a shudder.

"I think fishing sounds like a great idea," Sabrina said, appearing out of nowhere. "James, what do you say? You and Dad can spend some time together while Quinn and I take Mom out for a little girl time at the salon."

Seriously? What had he ever done to Sabrina? He looked pleadingly at Quinn again, waiting for the big excuse, the last-minute save that she usually came through with for him.

"I think that sounds like a great idea," Quinn said finally. "If James is up for it, of course."

Everyone was staring at him now. Quinn's mother with an expectant smile, Sabrina and Quinn with sly smiles that said they were enjoying this far too much, whereas Mr. Taylor glared at James like he was a leper invited to take a bath with him. James didn't see many choices here.

He forced a smile. "Would love to."

JAMES WAS COLD.

No, cold didn't even begin to cover it; his body felt like a popsicle dipped into an ice bath and left out to freeze against biting Arctic winds, winds that picked up speed as they swirled across the vast expanse of the lake's frozen surface.

He was in hell. They'd been here thirty minutes already, and James was certain he was in the early stages of hypothermia. The only thing more hellish than the temperatures were the smug grins that Bill Taylor and his buddies were giving him as they cracked open ice-cold beers and actually appeared like they were enjoying themselves. At his expense.

If James knew what was good for him, he'd have quit the minute they stepped out onto the ice and he'd heard what he swore was the sound of the ice cracking under his feet. But no, he was determined that no one—not the girls or their father—would get the better of him. Plus, he felt like he and Quinn's dad had gotten off on the wrong foot. For some reason, James found himself wanting the older man to like him. Or at least not think of him like he was a turd smeared on his shoe.

"Why don't you go check your line, James," Quinn's dad asked him. "Looks like you might have something."

James glanced down at his line that, in fact, was bobbing up and down on the stand as if something was on the other end. An unexpected thrill shot through him. Was he actually going to catch something?

He leaped forward with renewed energy and grabbed the line.

"Keep pulling. Don't give it any slack," Bill shouted as he and two of his friends surrounded him. "That's it. Now pull that in."

James could barely feel his fingers, but he somehow managed to hold on to the battling line, and he kept pulling the line, inch by inch, out of the water, waiting for that moment when the prized catch would finally come into view. This had to be worth some points, right? No one else had caught so much as a nibble all morning.

The line was biting into his hand as the blasted fish on the other end refused to come up willingly, and James's excitement climbed. This thing had to be huge if the fight it was giving was any indication.

It was almost too strong, and without thinking, he took a step, only to feel the ball of his foot sliding forward. Sharp, bone-sucking pain took his breath away as his leg went into the icy waters. His elbow slammed against the frozen surface as he sank almost to his right hip in the water.

Phew. His heart was racing as for a moment he'd thought he was going to sink entirely into the hole. From the stunned faces of the men around him, they'd thought the same thing. Hands were pulling him up, and as he gained his ground again, he looked down to see that, despite his brush with death, he'd managed not to release his grip on the line that was still tugging away.

"I still got it," he shouted.

This thing was not getting away. With even more determination, he pulled the line up again until, with one final tug that felt like it might have sapped the rest of his strength, his prey gave up as he yanked it from the water.

It was massive, at least one foot long and...

Purple?

He held up the line, trying to process what he was seeing. A purple fish that looked suspiciously like it was made of rubber.

James glanced up in confusion and saw the abashed grins of Bill and his friends. It only took him another second to realize that they'd played him, the end of the fish showing another line that someone—probably the men who were laughing uproariously thirty yards away—had been tugging on the entire time.

Bill was eying him with some guilt. "It's just an old trick, son. We didn't mean to have you nearly fall into the damn lake."

James stared at the sad, rubbery purple fish again and felt something other than anger tickle his chest as he thought about how ridiculous he must have appeared just moments ago.

His shoulders shook before he finally erupted into his own laughter. Because aside from the stinging pain along his right side that even now was feeling almost numb, the whole thing was actually kind of funny.

The other men joined in his laughter, Bill going so far as to wipe the tears from his eyes as he patted James on the back.

Almost making the whole thing worth it.

13

IT WAS close to noon when James and Quinn's dad arrived back home. Quinn, Sabrina, and their mom had barely beaten the men home, having spent their morning at the salon where Cindy was treated to some much-deserved pampering. Quinn and her sister were careful not to let anything slip out about the big surprise planned for that night. She only hoped that the other townspeople were as discreet.

With Sabrina holed up in her room writing, Quinn sat at the kitchen table having tea with her mom while trying not to worry what calamities might have befallen James out on the lake with her dad and his buddies. Her nerves calmed a little when the garage door opened and the Suburban pulled in.

Quinn would have smelled their arrival even if she hadn't heard them come into the kitchen a minute later. "Did someone fall in?" she asked. James didn't look wet, but the smell was definitely stronger in his direction.

"Just a little mishap with the bait," was all he said. Her dad chuckled.

Uh-oh. "Dad. You and your buddies didn't give James a hard time, did you?"

Crap. She couldn't explain what had overcome her this morning when she'd seen him standing there in another flannel shirt—blue this time—another day's growth on his chiseled jaw, and a grin that told her he was probably remembering how silly and immature she'd been the night before.

Which was why she'd needed some distance from him when she'd pushed him out the door with her dad. She'd also thought it might give the two men a chance to get to know each other and maybe let her dad see, as she had, that James wasn't quite the devil's spawn. She hadn't given any consideration to the possibility that her dad and his cronies might take the opportunity to play one of their usual pranks —on her boss. That was, if she hadn't been fired.

But James didn't seem annoyed or embarrassed by her dad's laughter, however, as he shrugged good-naturedly. "Let's just say it was all very instructive. In the meantime, I might take a long, hot shower. If you'll excuse me."

Quinn had to admit, for a man who was probably just hazed by her dad and his friends, he looked entirely too satisfied with himself as he strode down the hall.

"Bill," her mom said in a warning tone.

"What?" her dad asked, the picture of innocence. "You heard him. It was a mishap." He laughed again and grabbed a beer from the fridge before facing his wife. He paused, studying her. "Did you do something different with your hair?" he asked.

Whatever reprimand his wife was going to give him died on her lips, her hand rising to primp her hair. "Why, the girls thought that in addition to treating us to dinner tonight, they'd treat me to some pampering. Do you like it?"

"Like it? It's giving me all sorts of ideas," he said in a way that made Quinn want to hold her hands to her ears.

"Oh, which reminds me," her mom said, taking her gaze from her husband to settle on Quinn. "If James is going to be staying with us again, should we see if he'd like to come to dinner with us?"

"Sure, I'll let him know."

"I think I should probably shower off, too," her dad said, pulling on her mom's hand. "Did you want to help me find that shirt for later?"

Good grief. How had she and her sister survived their childhood without dying of mortification?

With the main room to herself, Quinn made a few more calls, confirming some questions with the caterer, then the florist, including whether the hydrangeas had arrived for the centerpieces. Hanging up a few minutes later, she looked at the last thing on her list. Finalizing the playlist for the DJ who they'd been lucky enough to find after the band confirmed now two members were sick.

"Has your father ever owned anything that didn't come in a plaid? Or flannel?" James asked, joining her in the kitchen. Sure enough, he was now sporting a blue-and-gray-plaid shirt and a pair of very worn Levi's. And even though the clothes might have originally been her dad's, James certainly managed to make them his own.

She felt the urge to retreat from the room on some flimsy excuse but stopped herself. This was her employer, and it would be best to clear the air now rather than later.

He came to stand next to her, smelling clean and delicious and uniquely James. "Whatcha doing?" he asked, seemingly unaware of his affect on her.

She glanced up. James was running his fingers through the short growth of his beard that was growing in nice and thick, and she wondered whether it was soft or prickly to the touch, her fingers itching to find out.

What had he asked her again?

Oh, that's right. "I'm about to finalize the playlist that the DJ emailed. I have no idea what Sabrina was thinking when she approved some of these," she said studying it again.

James leaned down far too close to read it. "It's not that bad."

"Justin Bieber? Ariana Grande? Yeah, sure, if you're at a prom or a dance club perhaps. But this is my parents' thirtieth wedding anniversary. I want the songs to mean something to them." She scrolled down to her music app and pulled it up. "I'm just going to have to put together something of my own."

James slid onto the barstool next to her. "I've got some time on my hands. Maybe we can come up with something together."

A door opened above them and Quinn knew her parents would be down shortly. Which meant they couldn't work here, not if they wanted to keep this thing a secret. Ordinarily, she'd head to her own bedroom where she could shut the door to keep their prying eyes out. But with James in tow and the only seating available being her bed, it wasn't an option.

"Follow me," she whispered and shut the laptop. Grabbing two throw blankets off the couch, she tossed them in James's direction before opening the sliding doors that led to the back yard and the guesthouse. Heat or not.

The snow was deeper here since Sabrina hadn't any reason to shovel the walkway now that she wasn't using the former boathouse, and Quinn labored to stick each step as they reached the door. Leaning down, she snagged the spare key left in a fake rock by the door, and let them inside.

Sabrina was right. With the furnace out, the place was colder than an icebox. But at least it was private and spacious and the bed wasn't the primary focus of the room.

"So this is Sabrina's digs?" he asked, looking around.

She nodded. "It was originally built as a boathouse, but my parents refurbished it, something that came in handy when Sabrina moved home a couple years ago."

The place was set up like a studio apartment with the living room area and it's couch and recliner the most prominent. Along one wall was a small kitchenette, with a half wall that separated it from the sleeping area in the corner. But it was the fireplace that Quinn was aiming for. "How are your fire-starting capabilities?"

"Is there a gas line?" he asked.

She was about to roll her eyes when she saw the teasing grin and familiar glint in his blue eyes.

"Here, allow me." He tossed the blankets to the couch and knelt down and sorted through the small pile of firewood. He stacked them and stuffed in a couple sheets of newspaper that were placed nearby before grabbing the torch lighter from the mantel and lighting it.

Not bad. In another minute, the fire had grown nicely. Quinn wrapped a dark gray blanket around her and sank onto the couch. Pulling her computer to her lap, she opened it again and punched in the password.

"Hey, do you think your sister will mind if I brew us some coffee?"

"You know how to brew a pot of coffee, too?"

Now he just looked exasperated. "You know, I'm not ten years old. I know how to drive a car, start a fire, make a pot of coffee, even brush my own teeth." He walked over to the small coffeepot and rinsed the carafe out before filling it with water. "What would you think if I went about making stereotypical assumptions about you because you're a woman or a lawyer? You'd jump down my throat in a minute."

She blinked. It was hard to admit, but he might have a point. "You're right. I'm sorry. I need to work on that."

He nodded and finished measuring the coffee and flipped on the brew button before coming back to join her. "What kind of music do your parents like? Let's see, thirty-year anniversary...that would mean they were married in the late eighties. That should make for an interesting compilation."

She clicked play on one song she knew was one of her parents' favorites. The opening tune of a Peter Cetera song. She grinned at him. "Dad took Mom to see *Karate Kid II* on their first date, and I guess this was on the soundtrack. It's kind of their song."

The song was beyond cheesy. All this talk about a man fighting for someone's honor? But Quinn had to admit that there was something about those very words that hit her in the heart when she heard it. Every time.

"Okay. Add it to the list. What's next? Actually, let me try one." He took the laptop and typed something in. "If we're choosing eighties love songs, this is sure to be a hit."

The artist's distinctive voice soared from the speakers. Whitney Houston singing about always loving someone.

"I don't know. I always thought that one was kind of sad. She's just going to pine away always remembering this great big love as they go on, living their separate lives? What was so insurmountable that they couldn't work out to be together?"

"Look at you." He was smiling and his eyes were soft as he stared at her. "The big romantic. Okay, how about this one?"

The next hour flew by as they added songs from The Cars, Depeche Mode, and Madonna to the growing list.

"Okay, so this one is a real oldie," James said, "but one of the few memories I have as a kid is my parents playing this song late at night when I was in my room trying to sleep."

This immediately sobered Quinn up. James had never talked about his parents before. Ever.

She knew the song. "I Only Have Eyes For You." It was a classic. Sweet and romantic, and she found herself content to just sit and listen to the words, noticing James sitting just as still.

"What a wonderful memory to have of your parents," she said when it finished, imagining a couple, maybe a man with eyes like James and a woman with his same easy grin, dancing late at night when they thought they were alone.

James didn't say anything, instead getting up to top off his coffee. He stood there, taking a sip. "I don't have a lot of memories of them, mostly just feelings whenever I think of them. One thing I'm certain of, they were very happy. Very much in love."

"They'd be proud of you, you know. At what you've accomplished." She had no idea where that had come from or whether it would be welcome. But something told her he didn't hear a lot of compliments and he was definitely due one.

"I'd like to think so." He shrugged. "How about your parents? I mean, we all know that our culture doesn't really look too kindly on lawyers anymore. Was your decision to go to law school a dream or nightmare to them?"

He was right about that. The jokes just never got old. "My mom would have been happy with whatever I decided to do. Being a teacher, anything that encouraged more learning was a plus for her. As to my dad, he was even more excited than I was when I got my acceptance letter. I think if things had been different, if he'd had the means and opportunity of going to college back then, he would have loved nothing more than becoming a litigator. And he would have been a good one, the best."

"I've no doubt," James said quickly. "Actually, I've always been a little curious. You attended Berkeley Law—not a shabby institution by any means—and you were on the *Law Review*, which would mean you must have been at the top of your class to earn such an honor. There must have been any number of high-paying jobs available to you. Top jobs at some of the biggest law firms in the country, I'd venture. So, how is it that when I met you, you were working at that tiny obscure law firm?"

"Now who's being a snob?" she said, trying to deflect the question. "Just because a firm doesn't have hundreds of associates and paralegals and doesn't bill millions of hours a year doesn't mean they're not first-rate."

"Of course it doesn't. But I find it hard to believe that, fresh out of law school, you hadn't set your sights on something a little more prestigious, such as working for a judge or some governmental agency."

She picked up her mug and finished off the last drink, buying a moment's time. "Well, I did actually. I had a job at this big, fancy law firm. Spencer Hautner. You might have heard of them." He nodded. "I clerked there after my second year of law school and was one of the few selected in their new associates program after I graduated."

"Now that makes sense," he said, nodding. "So what happened?"

Quinn took in a breath and slowly exhaled, trying to slow her rapidly beating heart. There was no shame, to her or her family, in what had happened. She knew that. But she did have a moment's qualm about sharing her mom's personal story like this.

But it was James. And she realized how much she wanted him to know, to understand.

"About three months after I started, my mom got into a pretty severe car accident. She fractured a couple of vertebrae, broke her left leg, had lacerations all over her face. It was bad. Her recovery took every single hour of her FMLA, not to mention, she was forced to exhaust her paid sick and vacation leave to cover her time off. But her back and her leg healed, the stitches and bruises disappeared, and for a time, we thought everything was going to be okay. She returned to work at the school, ready to get back into her regular routine. Only she started having these panic attacks. At first it was just about getting behind the wheel, something we could understand, and my dad was able to drop her off in the morning, and Sabrina usually picked her up. But then they occurred more frequently, for no reason, at night eating dinner, in the middle of the day grading papers sitting in her classroom, until one day she found herself sitting in a bathroom stall, shaking, trying to tell herself there was nothing to worry about. It got pretty bad up until she—she was admitted to the hospital and she was finally diagnosed with PTSD."

"PTSD?" His brows furrowed. "Isn't that like what soldiers who've been in war suffer?"

She nodded. "They do, but anyone who's suffered a significant trauma can experience it, too. In my mom's case, she had a history of anxiety and depression, so they think she was just more prone to experiencing it after her accident. I say *think* because, like all these illnesses, there's no absolute clear diagnosis. But their assessment and resulting treatment seemed to help her get her symptoms and her anxiety under control. Unfortunately, when she returned to work at the school this time, the district and superintendent weren't as sympathetic. In fact, they were paranoid that one little thing might set her off and make her a danger to her students."

Something caught in her voice at this and she stopped.

Her sweet, kind mother was considered a risk, someone to be afraid of by people who'd known her for years. She'd had to ask her treating doctor to write a detailed letter assuring them that she wasn't a risk to anyone—that had been the most humiliating and infuriating moment.

"It crushed my mom especially when every tiny infraction with a student was scrutinized from the viewpoint that maybe she'd been somehow to blame. It got to be too much for her. She finally took an early retirement last year."

"That's ridiculous. Your mom has got to be the most genuine and kindest person I've met." James shook his head, looking nearly as angry as she'd felt when it happened. "That's horrible. And you quit your job then? Is that what happened? To take care of her?"

This was where things got a little more...real. Her stomach was in knots as she wrestled with whether to tell him everything. But this was James and right now, she wanted—no needed—him to know all there was to know about her.

She inhaled a shaky breath. Good and bad.

14

JAMES COULD SEE that Quinn was struggling with something, and he waited, patiently, giving her the time she needed to get it out. Why she quit what had to be a high paying job, one so needed with her mom's bills looming over her.

She sighed, fidgeting with the strings on the corner of her blanket. "After the accident, my parents were hit with astronomical medical bills. Not just for the car accident but for Mom's psychiatric admission later on. The only reason Sabrina and I knew about it was because she overheard my dad on the phone talking to someone about their options, options that included taking a second mortgage on the house or declaring bankruptcy. So Sabrina and I talked about it and came up with our own plan. I approached my dad and told him I had this massive sign-on bonus at my job, not to mention a triple-digit salary, and I talked him into letting me pay for everything. As I told him, it was the least I could do for them after everything they've done for me, helping me when they could during college. Of course, as a first-year associate, I had no such thing. But I took out a loan and Sabrina moved back home to help out and started writing her novels. We were able to get by."

His brows furrowed as he processed that. The sacrifice she had made as well as her sister for their parents. It humbled him to think they would give up so much for someone they loved. He didn't think he'd ever experienced that. "So that explains the reason you needed the job so badly. Your mom's medical bills."

"Yes, not to mention my monstrous student loan payments that came due around the same time. Which actually is what brings me to why I left Spencer Hautner." She tightened the blanket around her shoulders, seeking their warmth from the sudden chill. "Like I said, my mom had a family history of depression and anxiety that had gone undiagnosed until her breakdown. And as I was soon to discover with the added stress from my own bills and mom's uncertain mental health, I shared the same predisposition. Don't worry, it never got as bad as with my mom where I needed to be hospitalized," she rushed to assure him, as if that was even a passing consideration for him, his heart aching so much for her. "But I was finding that working sixty-hour workweeks to keep up my billable hours was taking a toll. So with my roommates' help, I found this woman, a therapist who I could talk to. And with the antidepressants I started taking, things improved to some degree, but I was still overwhelmed and completely miserable. I needed to make a change. I saw that Meiers and Rooney was hiring an associate for their caseload, which included employment discrimination cases much like my mom's, and they were more than happy to give me a try. So I quit. And although the financial stress didn't ease—especially since the healthcare package wasn't quite as generous as at

Spencer Hautner—my happiness, my job satisfaction, was immeasurable."

During her recitation, Quinn had been careful to keep her gaze from his, even now repositioning the blanket around her for a distraction.

"So there you have it," she said, forcing a smile. "Why cases like Laurie's and my mom's have a special interest to me. Why I want to help those employees, make sure they're provided the rights and accommodations they're legally entitled to."

"And your work at Thornhill, are you finding it rewarding? Is it making you happy?" he asked, his voice low and strangely hoarse. Because he'd hate to think that working at Thornhill—and with him—was another added stress. That she was...miserable. It was the last thing he wanted for her.

She considered his question for a moment "Sure, there are times when it feels like I'm working against a broken system. But I know that by being there, I'm slowly making changes for the better. Starting with the manager training sessions, and the EAP that's so close to becoming a reality."

James squirmed, knowing that now would be a good time to tell her what was going on back at the office. The concern that their bankers were suddenly expressing from out of nowhere, concerns involving the EAP.

Quinn took in another shaky breath, deciding to try for humor to break the gravity that had settled over them. "But I promise, I'm not going to go postal on you."

"Of course you're not," he almost snapped, not so much because she'd offended him, but because he knew that other people might have that ridiculous notion pass their own narrow-minded brains. James rose from his spot on the couch and came to kneel in front of her, taking the laptop from her and setting it down before he rested his hand over hers.

He studied her, forcing her to meet his gaze. "If I haven't said this before, let me be clear now. You are one of the most driven, bright, and passionate people I know, Quinn Taylor. The fact that you take medicine to combat your condition is no different to me than someone who takes insulin for diabetes or statins to combat high cholesterol. It's not who you are, it's just something you have. You shouldn't feel ashamed. If anything, you should be proud of yourself, for doing what you knew was right in helping your folks, for stepping away from a high-paying prestigious job—which couldn't have been easy for anyone—because you knew it was the right choice for you and the people you want to help. People like your mom and Laurie. I have only the utmost admiration and respect for you."

Quinn swallowed, her dark brown eyes wide and filled with a flood of tears. Tears he'd never seen her shed before. She blinked and one slipped slowly down her cheek.

"Damn. I'm sorry," she said, brushing it away. "I don't cry. Crying is a sign of weakness. And I don't cry in front of the boss."

That ripped at his heart. "First, crying is far from a sign of weakness. It's a sign of being human. Of having a heart. A soul. And second..." He smiled, reaching out to stop her from brushing another tear away, his thumb gently brushing away the wetness from her cheek. "I hope I'm more to you than just your boss. I'd like to believe that we're friends, and maybe even—"

He stopped, his emotions so raw that he didn't know exactly what he wanted or what he risked saying.

Quinn was so close. Dangerously close. Her eyes widened, as she seemed to become aware of this, too. Dark, brown eyes that were often filled with frustration, or anger, and sometimes laughter when they were together were now filled with something else entirely.

Something that looked distinctly like passion. Desire. Need. Her gaze dropped to stare at his lips, and she licked her own almost nervously. Any flashing warning signs that should have been blazing at what he was about to do, were strikingly absent. Because this was right. Right and a long time coming.

James leaned forward, inch by inch, so she would know what was about to happen and had time to withdraw if she needed to.

But she didn't move. Instead, her mouth opened.

And he was lost.

IT HAPPENED SO NATURALLY, the way his lips pressed to hers, feather-light, almost like a caress that sent a tingling sensation over her skin, that Quinn didn't have time to consider whether this was the rational thing to be doing.

She'd just caught her breath when his lips returned again, the pressure harder, and she closed her eyes against the heady sensation of firm, warm lips, of a strong hand that cupped the back of her head, drawing her in so that his tongue was able to taste her more fully. His beard was soft but also bristly against her mouth, especially when he deepened the kiss. She caressed her tongue against his, aware of a sighing noise that slipped from the back of her throat.

Then he was kissing her chin and the crevice of her neck, his beard almost rough now against the tender skin but, when combined with the sensual kissing, felt exquisite. The blanket had fallen away from her, and as James leaned forward, sinking with her against the couch, she instinctively wrapped her legs around him. He was so warm and strong and like everything she ever could have wanted as she clung to him.

All her fears that he could never see her as a woman he'd want in his arms, want to kiss like this, had been unfounded. James wanted her, flaws and all.

A feeling of joy and relief and excitement soared through her. This man, this amazing man, wanted her, despite what she'd told him about herself. It was the only thing she cared about as she pushed any other doubts or worries away and just lost herself in this moment.

This kiss.

The rattling sound of someone trying to open the front door was like a bucket of cold water dumped on them both as they bolted upright. James jumped to his feet, grabbing his coffee mug, as Quinn sat up and tried to smooth her hair.

But something still felt off. It was only as the door swung open to reveal Sabrina standing there looking entirely too smug did Quinn realize that somehow James had somehow managed to unclasp the back of her bra. How had he done that so quickly?

"Sorry to interrupt, but it's almost two, and we're supposed to be leaving for the hall to help with the decorations."

Quinn tried to smile easily, even as the skin around her mouth still tingled and she had some suspicions as to its redness caused by James's kisses. "No problem. James and I were just putting the finishing touches on the playlist for the DJ tonight."

"Oh, really? How did that go?" Sabrina asked in a tone that suggested some doubt in her sister's story.

"We think your parents will find the selection pretty inspired," James added from the kitchenette, where he'd gone to rinse out his cup. "Nice place you got here."

"I like it. In fact, with the isolation, the wood-burning fire, the dim lighting, it's pretty inspiring for writing sexy love stories."

Quinn ignored her sister's comment and slipped her feet back into her boots and stood, tucking her laptop under her arm. "I'm all set. Maxine should have the flowers already delivered, the caterers should also be there getting things set up, and the cake will be there by four."

"Did you want to tag along, James? Maybe give us a hand with the preparations?"

"No!" Quinn said a little too sharply before taking a steadying breath. She needed some space and some time away from James to try and figure out what had just happened and what it might mean. "James was just mentioning how, if he was sticking around for the party tonight, he needed something other than plaid or flannel. Wasn't that right?" She didn't give him a chance to answer as she continued. "You can take old Bessie when you're ready to head back into town. Sabrina and I will take the parents' Suburban. We can meet up later."

James smiled easily, not appearing the least alarmed by what had just happened between them. Quite the contrary. "Sure, no problem. I have some calls to make anyhow. We'll catch up tonight."

There was a definite gleam in his eyes and she wondered what he must think of her, of what they'd done.

Fricking-A. What the heck had just come over them? Over her? They'd kissed.

No...they'd freaking made out like a couple of teenagers. Her boss had felt her up. Fresh horror and embarrassment flooded her face, and she kept her gaze down as she met Sabrina at the door.

"Should we stop at the house and make up some excuse for Mom and Dad?" Sabrina asked.

"Not unless you want a repeat of Easter 2009."

"Hmm. Must be something genetic."

Quinn looked sharply at her sister, who only smiled angelically while staring pointedly down at Quinn's chest where the soft cups of her bra had bunched up, making it pretty clear it was no longer clasped.

"See you later, James," Sabrina added more brightly.

"Looking forward to it."

Only it sounded more like a promise, and despite the new anxiety gripping her, Quinn shivered in anticipation.

Almost on autopilot, James pulled Bessie into the open parking spot in front of the outfitter store and put the truck in park as the refrain that had been echoing in his mind for the past ten minutes continued.

He'd kissed her.

He, James Thornhill, had kissed Quinn Taylor.

Not just any kiss. But one that was so hot and so intense that it kept playing over again in his mind. Her warm, sweet mouth that had tasted like coffee and honey, the way her dark, silky hair had felt in his fingers, the feeling of her body responding so wholeheartedly and unexpectedly to his, the way she moaned so softly and almost drove him insane with desire.

James ran a tremulous hand over his face, stopping to splay in the soft hair of his beard, something that he seemed to notice Quinn had liked as well.

Damn it. He had to stop thinking about that moment if he was going to be able to function.

If anything, what he should be thinking about right now wasn't about all the things he'd have loved to do with Quinn Taylor had her sister not interrupted them, but coming up with a way out of the crisis going on back at Thornhill that was going to blow everything up.

The fact that the bank that was just short of underwriting the biggest deal James had put together, a deal that would bring the Blossom Brew franchise to Thornhill Management was now balking.

According to the guy he'd talked to, it wasn't so much that the company was adding an employment assistance plan to the current health benefit package, as it was that, in the short-run, it was bound to be an additional financial burden that had to be taken into consideration when they assessed the bottom line, the profits. Their question to James had been whether Thornhill was stretching itself out too thin in such a short space of time.

A question he had adamantly denied. But he was also sure that something else was up with this, that someone back at the office was saying something contrary to what James was asserting.

What he should be doing is finding the next flight out of here, forget his plane, his trip to Cabo—a trip that he no longer even thought about—and forget sharing another private intimate moment with Quinn. Because if this wasn't fixed, and the EAP was no longer on the table, there wouldn't be any more moments with her. And that was something he would avoid at all costs.

Even if that risk meant him losing this deal? Losing the one chance he had to prove to his grandfather that he could be relied on? That trusting in James to run the company he'd built hadn't been a mistake?

James prayed it would never come to that, having already sent to the bank the same PowerPoint that Quinn had put together to convince Thornhill's board. If she could convince those stodgy old men on the board that the EAP was sound, she could certainly convince a bunch of bankers.

There was one thing that he needed to take care of.

Acting on his hunch, James saw the necessary bars on his cell phone and pressed send, waiting for the man to answer.

"Dennis. It's James," he said when the man answered. "I've been talking to the bank, trying to resolve some sudden concerns they're expressing. You wouldn't know anything about that would you?

"I know everything where it concerns this company, James," the man threw out in a condescending tone. "It's the reason I've been your grandfather's right-hand man for more than thirty years."

"It's been that long, huh? Well then maybe you can tell why this has suddenly turned into a bigger issue that it was, say, three days ago, when I was in town and we were close to signing off on the whole thing."

"Well, as the General Counsel for the company, I felt it was my legal and moral obligation to share with them some concerns that I and a few other members of the board were having about so many changes, so much money going out and no sure signs it would ever come back."

It was as James has suspected. Dennis was trying to sabotage the deal.

And it was the last damn straw.

"Of course. You got to do what you got to do, right? I kind

of feel the same way. In fact, let me just say that I really appreciate the time you've put into this company—at least when the company's needs didn't usurp your ego. But I don't think that we're on the same page as to where I envision this company will be going in the next ten, twenty years. To make this easier on everyone, I'm going to offer you a nice voluntary retirement package of, say, twenty-five percent of your annual salary. Now, you can take that offer and walk away, or you can wait until Monday, when I fire your ass and you're left with nothing."

There was a hissing sound at the other end, and James waited for the explosion.

"You think you have that kind of power, boy? You think you have the votes you need on this issue? You don't know who you're messing with. I'm not going anywhere. My removal takes more than just your say so."

"I beg to differ. I am still the acting CEO of this company, and until the board sees fit to vote me out of that position, I make the final calls regarding hiring and firing of employees. And with this lucrative deal that I'm bringing to the table, and the anticipated profit that each of those board members will see in their pockets in the coming months and years, I think they're going to give me the benefit of the doubt to steer this company as I see fit. So I'd start dusting off my resume if I were you, Dennis."

With that, James hung up, feeling a hundred percent lighter with his decision. No regrets.

Actually, come to think of it, he had no regrets at all about where things were going in his life, both business-related, and...personal. Particularly personal. Because despite his usual tendency to jump ship with any woman when things were starting to feel as good as they did with Quinn, he didn't want to go anywhere.

Sure. He was ready to jump all right. But jump with her, and enjoy the fall as they went.

He looked at the time. Enough of ruminating. He had a party to get ready for and a woman to convince they needed to do a lot more kissing.

15

"I DON'T UNDERSTAND why you girls parked two blocks away from the restaurant when I'm certain that we could have found something much closer," Quinn's mom said as they walked down the sidewalk, nearly to the actual destination of the Elks Club.

"I'm just anticipating that when we leave the restaurant, I'm going to be so stuffed I'll need the extra steps," Sabrina said, in a lame attempt to deflect further questions on their parking choice.

Quinn didn't say anything as the conversation continued around her. It had been something of a relief when James texted them an hour ago to say he was wrapping some things up and would meet them at the party, giving her a reprieve from the inevitable discussion they needed to have.

But as every step brought her closer to seeing that handsome face, those twinkling blue eyes, and a smile that would undoubtedly send her heart thumping against her chest, she grew more nervous.

What on earth had James been thinking when he kissed

her? And what the heck had she been thinking when she kissed him back?

And just like the dozens of times she'd analyzed this in the past few hours, she reached the same conclusion.

It had been a mistake. Plain and simple.

One just didn't get involved in that way with one's boss. Ever. Not only was it unprofessional but it would also call into question her credibility when she drove home the importance to the managers during her legal training that their employees were not to be used as their personal dating pool. And knowing James Thornhill as she did, a break-up was inevitability, since serial dating was all he was capable of. And Quinn refused to be his flavor of the week, something she would tell him at the next opportunity.

That was, if he even remembered the whole thing. For all she knew, the kiss was just a one-off thing anyhow, not having any particular importance. Something that—even if she didn't want anything more herself—would still have a particular sting.

As they rehearsed, her sister stopped suddenly and read a text from her phone. "Shoot."

"What's the matter?" their dad asked.

"It's from Lindsey. She's in charge of the family bingo night, and they ran into some trouble with a pipe bursting. They had to move everything to the Elks Club at the last minute. Only they can't get the circuit breaker to flip. Do you think you'd mind stopping for a minute, Dad, to see if you can pinpoint the problem?" She pointed ahead. "It's just half a block up."

"Of course, but I've been telling Marv Gillis for the past six years that that circuit was a hazard and they needed to replace it."

Quinn and Sabrina smothered their smiles as they followed behind.

The lights were on outside the place, but when Sabrina opened the door, everything inside was dark.

"You sure they said the Elks Hall—" her dad started.

The lights flipped on and the chorus of "surprise!" from their guests filled the air. Her mom and dad stood there, mouths open as they took a few seconds to process and realize that it was all for them.

Quinn laughed and joined Sabrina in hugging them. "It's a surprise party, guys. We wanted to celebrate your special day with a big party."

The shock was wearing off, as her mom got misty-eyed, turning to give each daughter a long hug. "You girls didn't have to—" But she got choked up and stopped.

Fortunately, the people who'd been waiting for them in the hall no longer were holding back as they surrounded the happy couple with well wishes. It was hard for Quinn not to jerk her head around, trying to find one familiar face in particular, since something told her that he was already there, maybe watching her now. A possibility that had her already-racing pulse going into overdrive.

"I'm going to go check on the caterers," she said to her sister. "Make sure everything is okay. Could you see if the DJ is ready to go?"

"I will. But then you need to relax and have fun. Look around," Sabrina said gazing upward.

Quinn followed her gaze to the fairy lights and paper lanterns that were strung across the ceiling, setting everything awash in a soft, romantic glow. The table settings were gorgeous, made more perfect by the floral centerpieces that included both the white hydrangeas *and* pink peonies—

something she'd have to thank Maxine for later. It was perfect.

"We did all this," Sabrina said, turning back to her. "Now you need to trust that everything is going to work out. Deal?"

Before Quinn could nod her agreement, she spotted James standing about ten feet away from them, grinning at her in that confident, sexy way that left her head spinning.

He looked good. Sinfully good, as he well knew. Even here in the middle of nowhere, he'd managed to get his hands on a light gray suit that seemed to be made for those broad shoulders and his tall athletic frame. Combined with loafers, he was back to looking like the debonair playboy CEO that she'd been trying not to think salacious thoughts about for months.

Except for the beard. Which, for some reason, having just felt it caressing her skin hours before, made James almost feel more like hers.

He pushed his hands in his pockets and sauntered over.

"I'll go check on the DJ while you..." Sabrina trailed off when he approached and she smiled slyly. "Actually, James, I'm trusting you will make sure that my sister chills for a little while? Maybe actually has a good time?"

"I'll do my best."

Only he hadn't taken his eyes off her, and she was finding that if he didn't stop staring at her like he was undressing her with his eyes, she was probably going to melt into the floor at his feet. With a knowing smile, Sabrina was off, leaving Quinn trying to remember what it meant to form coherent speech.

"You're stunning."

She licked her lips, her throat suddenly dry.

And she tried to remember all the reasons why anything

more than a professional relationship with James Thornhill was impossible. When right now, it seemed more than just possible.

It seemed inevitable.

JAMES TRIED to take in a breath, but for a moment, it was like he'd forgotten how.

Yes, Quinn was beautiful. There was no denying that as she stood before him now in that dead-sexy dress that tantalized him with a glimpse of the tops of her breasts, her hair flowing down her left shoulder, so thick and lustrous, and he wanted to run his fingers through it nearly as much as he wanted to kiss the pout off those full red lips that even now she was licking almost nervously. However, she'd also appeared no less beautiful to him this morning, without any makeup and covered head-to-toe in jeans and a long-sleeved sweater.

If he were being honest with himself, even before he'd pulled up at her house yesterday morning to begin this little journey, he'd already spent too much time wondering about Quinn and what was going on in that brilliant head of hers. Like why did she insist on hiding behind those absurd glasses, or whether her lips would taste like chocolate and peanut butter just like the candies she hid from him, or something darker and more sinful.

"So, do you think we surprised them?" Quinn asked, ignoring his compliment just as she was avoiding his gaze.

Probably for the best because he was afraid if she saw into his eyes everything he was thinking she might run in the other direction. "I think that's a safe bet."

"Quinn," said a heavily perfumed woman who came up

behind them. "You and Sabrina really did a fabulous job here."

"Thank you, Aunt Chrissy. And thank you for all of the photos you sent. They were perfect for the tabletops." The woman's attention was on him, though, her expression curious. "Oh, I'm sorry, this is James Thornhill. My boss back in California."

She smiled, her curiosity turning to a suspicious gleam. "Nice to meet you, James. I'm terribly sorry to have just barged in on you two, but Quinn's great aunt Trudy and all of her kids are here and wanted to say hello. It shouldn't take long, but she wanted to make sure she had a chance to see her niece before things got too crazy."

"By all means. We'll catch up later," James promised to Quinn. Whether she liked it or not, he wanted to add. He smiled and enjoyed the flush of color that once again filled her face.

Only later turned out much longer that he anticipated as every time he spotted Quinn, she was surrounded by some well-meaning friend or family member who wanted to catch up on every minute of her life from the past ten years. James hadn't minded at first, studying his usually prickly attorney, now all smiles and laughter, the picture of relaxation as she caught up with people who obviously cared about her. But after an hour of this, he noticed that her shoulders were wilting and her smile was withering; she needed rescuing.

Stopping off at the buffet table where he loaded up a plate with all the delicacies he knew she'd like, along with a couple glasses of wine, he deposited everything at an empty table in the corner and set out to find Quinn.

A-ha. Over at the cake table chatting with a tall older blonde. As he drew closer, James recognized Quinn's fake smile pinned in place, a trapped expression in those brown eyes. "There you are," he said, noting her relief as she saw him. "You know, your sister gave me one task tonight, and that was to make sure that you took a moment to yourself and tried to eat something, which I know for a fact you haven't done."

"You're right," she said, her smile now grateful as she saw him. "And I'm afraid if I don't get a bite, I might pass out pretty soon. Deb, I think you've probably heard about James, my boss. And James, this is Deb. You met her daughter, Shelby, last night?"

Ah. The mother of the evil former best friend.

"Shelby said you were quite the looker and I have to say I whole-heartedly agree," Deb said, smiling brightly at him. "I don't want to keep Quinn any longer, since I know she worked so hard to pull this off. You two go eat while I find your mother so I can tell her how many times I almost spilled the beans about this whole thing."

"Shelby's mom, huh? Interesting," James said, taking Quinn's arm and guiding her through the room, making sure to keep a wide berth from any potential well-intentioned chatterboxes.

"To be fair, Deb is actually a very nice lady. But right now I can only take so many stories about how precocious and endearing her grandkids are and how lucky she is to have her daughter settled so close without wanting to smash my head into something."

"I'm glad I arrived when I did then." James slid her chair out, and then took his own after she was seated. He pushed her food toward her.

"Thank you," she said, and speared a forkful of macaroni salad.

Overhead, Rick Springfield's "Jessie's Girl," started playing and James smiled as he remembered how much fun they'd had selecting it. Although not quite as fun as when they'd kissed.

If Quinn was feeling similarly reminiscent, she hid it as she finished another bite, her attention on the plate. "Did you hear anything from your pilot? Weren't they supposed to have that part in this afternoon?"

He nodded. "The part has been received and, last I heard, everything should be ready by morning. Why? Are you trying to get rid of me?"

She glanced up at him for a nanosecond. "Frankly? Yes. Actually, now that you brought it up, I think now is a good time to talk about what happened. Before."

"Before?" he asked, pretending confusion.

Quinn shook her head. "You know exactly what I'm talking about."

He grinned. "Ah. You must be talking about the events that were taking place just before your sister so conveniently interrupted us. When you kissed me."

"Shh." She glanced around a little wildly. "Keep it down. Do you want someone to hear you? Wait." She seemed to have processed what he'd said. "I didn't kiss you. You kissed me."

He thought about it. "No, I don't know if that's what happened. Maybe you could tell me in detail what you remember transpiring."

"Yeah, I bet you'd like that." Only she was smiling at him, not appearing annoyed. "For the purpose of this conversation, let's agree that there was a kiss. A mutually acted upon kiss."

"Okay. I'm with you."

"And although said kiss was pretty good, I think we can both agree that it was also a mistake. And that out of respect to our future business relationship, we won't be doing any more kissing or anything else that would jeopardize that."

"Why?"

"Why? Are you seriously asking me that? Because—"

She stopped, and it was hard to miss the way she was staring at his lips before she realized what she was doing and turned quickly away. He had to work not to laugh.

She tried again. "Because I work for you. You're my boss. Anything beyond that would be highly inappropriate. One does not just kiss their boss."

He smiled at her puritanical ethics. "Ordinarily, I might agree with you. As a blanket statement, that's a practical and reasonable business policy. Especially coming from the woman who trains our managers on this very thing. But, you and I? We're an exception."

She snorted. "That's what every one says who dates their boss and later lives to regret it. James, we're not different. I know you, and I know how you operate. Dating a lot of different women is your M.O., and a three-day weekend in Napa is your idea of long-term commitment. And I'm not about to risk my job and my reputation for a flash-in-the-pan affair that, when you've moved on, will make me the office joke."

"You could never be a joke," James said and leaned forward, moving his hand close to hers so that their fingertips almost touched. "We are different, Quinn. Which is exactly why I'm ready to take this risk with you. Because I know that being with you will be different than all the other women in my life, none of whom have ever made me feel half of what I already feel for you. And if you decide that you can't accept the risk of seeing where this thing can go, nothing will change in your position with the company. With how I see you or treat you. But why should the fact that my name is just a couple of people above yours in the company hierarchy stop us from seeing just how good we could be together?"

"You have to stop talking like this, James. It's—it's just not going to happen."

"Because I'm your boss," he said, not disguising his frustration.

"Yes, because you're my boss. And have you thought for one second about the possibility that I—I just don't feel the same way about you?"

Now he did laugh, a warm chuckle. "Not possible."

Her eyes darkened. "Oh, really? You're so certain you're God's gift to women you can't imagine that any woman would actually not be interested in you? Well, you're going to be disappointed. I don't feel that way about you." But instead of meeting his gaze, she'd cast her eyes down again, as she usually did when she was holding something from him.

"I don't buy that for one minute," he said softly. "Not after today. Not after how you responded to me. Did you know that you make a soft moaning sound and you curl your toes when I kiss you"—he leaned forward, reaching his hand out to touch the area just under her jaw—"here? Or"—he slowly dropped his finger lower, caressing her skin —"here. And that before your sister decided to crash the party, you were biting that lip just like you're doing now as I brushed my hand across—"

"Mom. Dad," she said quickly, her eyes round as saucers as she gazed somewhere over his shoulder.

He hoped she was kidding. That this was just an attempt to make him sweat.

"Hey, pumpkin," said the gruff voice. "Your mother and I

just wanted to come over and tell you how much we appreciate what you did for us tonight."

If Quinn's dad had witnessed his caressing the man's daughter, James would be landing flat on his back right now, right? The dim lighting gave him a lot to be grateful for.

Cindy leaned down and hugged her daughter. "Everything is just perfect. The flowers, the cake, and the decorations. And this music. All my favorites."

"I'm happy you like it. Sabrina and I both worked hard to make this a success for you two."

"You did great, sweetie. And I insist that you sit back and enjoy the rest of the night. Deb already assured me that they have a cleanup crew ready first thing in the morning. In the meantime—" Cindy looked back at her husband as an Ed Sheeran song began—"Your dad and I are going to do a little dancing."

It was hard to miss the love in the older couple's eyes as they stared at each other and headed out to the floor. Even after thirty years. And James knew that no matter what Quinn may think about their chances, he knew that they could have that. They could have thirty, forty, hopefully even fifty years of similar love and laughter.

He just needed to convince Quinn to give them a chance.

James met her gaze again. Only instead of the somberness he expected to see, he found her biting back laughter, her eyes shining at him. She lasted another second before she giggled.

He smiled, willing to humor her. "Something funny?"

"Your. Face." She leaned over, holding her belly. "You looked positively terrified when you heard my parents were behind you. Your eyes—" She did what he could only assume was an imitation of him as her eyes widened like they were going to pop from her face and her mouth dropped open.

He was pretty certain he hadn't looked *that* bad. "Laugh it up while you can, because as soon as you've caught your breath, we're going to continue where we left off."

That seemed to do the trick, as almost instantly she sobered. "It's no use, James. Even if I enjoyed that moment on the couch, I wasn't thinking straight. Neither of us was. Because you and me? Even if you weren't my boss, and even if you weren't a known playboy who just can't help himself from playing the field. The idea of you and I as a couple would be ridiculous. We have nothing in common."

"That's not true. Just because we grew up differently, both had different experiences, that doesn't mean we don't have thinks in common. Because at our core, you and I, Quinn Taylor? We're the same. We value hard work, integrity, rewarding and protecting the employees who make businesses like Thornhill grow and thrive. We value honesty and respect. And most of all, underneath this crazy physical and emotional attraction we have for each other, we have a real friendship. One that I would never do anything to risk losing. I want you in my life, Quinn. I want you in my life because I know that together we could be really really good. And...happy."

Her lips had parted, and she seemed to be still processing this as her dark, brown eyes studied him almost fearfully. As if she wanted to believe him. Wanted to believe this could happen.

"I'm not saying we have to march into the office Monday morning locked in some public display of affection. We can act much like we do now. But at the end of the day, I don't want to say good night at the door of my office and have to wait to see you the next morning or the next week. I want to be able to pick you up at your place and take you out properly. When we eat at a restaurant, I want to take your hand whenever I want. To reach out and kiss those lips even when they're laughing at me. We could be really good together if you let us happen."

"I want to believe that could be true," she said almost breathlessly. "I want to believe everything you say."

"Then do it. Trust me, Quinn. Trust in us."

James didn't ordinarily believe in fate, but when the song ended and the next one on the list began to play, one that she must have added without him noticing, he knew without any doubt it had always been meant to be this way.

He came to his feet, sure now of everything, as he held his hand out to her. "Will you dance with me?"

She hesitated the barest of moments and he felt a moment of dread that everything he'd said had been for naught. That she was going to say no.

Then in a beautiful almost miraculous moment, she nodded and smiled, a smile of hope and acceptance before she placed her hand into his. James had never felt so overwhelmed with happiness and gratitude that she was willing to take this risk on him. No, on them. And he moved with her to the center of the dance floor, aware of the fairy lights above them glimmering just like they were the stars in the song that was playing.

She felt so incredibly soft and smelled so damn good it took everything he had to remember to move his feet for a moment. But then they were dancing, finally, and he wasn't looking anywhere but at her. Into those dark eyes that seemed to reflect his own terror and excitement at what was happening between them.

He never wanted to let her go.

16

THE MOMENT that Quinn placed her hand into James's, she had known what that meant, what it signified, and most importantly, what she wanted to do next with the man who had her believing for the first time in a long time that maybe a happily ever after was in the cards for her.

And now, as they walked hand in hand into the frigid quiet coldness of the guest house, the only place that would afford them the privacy she so desperately sought, she knew what was coming and she was gripped by anxiety and terror and excitement all rolled into one.

While James set to building up a fire to take the cold edge from the air, Quinn found matches and made her way around the room, lighting the candles that her sister seemed to have in ample supply. Ambiance, she'd once told Quinn in explanation, for the romance stories she was writing.

To keep busy, she grabbed the blankets she'd brought from the house earlier today and spread them on the floor, adding pillows, couch cushions, and even her sister's heavy duvet from her bed to make them a warm soft place for...

Quinn flushed at her thoughts. Was she really standing

here? Was she really going to do what she'd imagined for so long but had always dismissed as pure irrational fantasy? Was she really about to take the next steps into something that would be impossible to go back from with the man standing a few feet away from her?

Dear God, she hoped so.

The fire crackled and she turned, her heart beating like a drum in her chest as she looked up to find James studying her. There was a promise of sensuality and seduction in those blue cobalt eyes, and an intensity that was making it difficult for her to breathe.

This was definitely going to change things.

If James had any doubt about what they were about to do, he didn't show it as he took another step closer and reached out, caressing her face. She leaned into his hand, amazed at how such a simple touch could make her feel so much safer.

"Quinn, look at me." She hadn't even realized she'd closed her eyes but swept them open to find him studying her. "I want you to know something. This...this thing between us? It's real. What I feel for you is real. I would never do anything to hurt you. Do you trust me?"

She nodded, unable to find any words. Still waiting for the moment that she woke up.

Her gaze dropped to his mouth, and her lips almost tingled in anticipation of feeling his again. She didn't have to wait long as he finally leaned down, kissing her softly again. She leaned into him, the last of her doubts already slipping away.

James Thornhill, the enigmatic CEO who she'd been trying to fight her feelings for from almost the moment she'd seen him, acting all authoritative and yet also cheeky as he stood in front of the lawyers at their first meeting.

Here. Wanting her as much as she wanted him. Making her feel like he was the one who was lucky for having her.

Closing her eyes again, she embraced him whole-heartedly, knowing that come what may, after this was all over, having him, having this moment, was going to be worth it.

IT WAS WELL past midnight when, tucked under the covers and cozy and warm from the chill of the night, James settled his weight on one arm and faced her. He reached out, tucking a strand of hair behind her ear as he looked down at her, smiling. "I always knew it would be like this with you."

"Always knew?" she asked, raising a brow. "Exactly how long have you been imagining this?"

"The more appropriate question might be, when haven't I?"

Quinn laughed, as she reached up to run her fingers through his hair. "Maybe as long as I've wanted to do that."

"How have I never known this?"

"I have a few secrets of my own."

"Intriguing." He leaned down to kiss her, and then came to his feet to put a couple more logs on the fire. He could sense her watching him, something that gave him a strange sense of pleasure, almost as much as when she'd brushed her hand through his hair. "If you don't stop staring, you're going to make me blush."

"Please," she said, guffawing. "You're not capable of feeling embarrassment."

"Probably not." Returning to the floor, he pulled her against him and settled the blanket around them, enjoying how she leaned her head back against his shoulder.

"I wish we could stay in this moment forever."

He kissed the top of her head. "This is the first moment of many, many more."

"Well, except that you're going to Mexico in the morning."

"Actually, that's something I wanted to talk to you about. The exotic climes of Mexico don't seem nearly as enticing as remaining here with you. That is, if you can stand me for a couple more days. We can fly out on Sunday night together. Unless you think your father might be meeting me in the morning with the barrel of a shotgun pointed at me."

"I think my dad is long past needing to protect my honor," she said, smiling. "As to your sticking around, I can't think of anything I'd like more. You haven't experienced the full Taylor experience until you've had at least one of mom's home-cooked meals."

Exactly what he wanted to hear. "Then we wouldn't want to disappoint her." He leaned down, nuzzling her neck. "But in the meantime, there's a lot of hours between now and breakfast, and I can think of a few things we can do to pass the time."

As ways to wake up went, having the soft backside of a beautiful woman pressed up against him was unbeatable. He lifted his head, watching her for a moment as she slept. All vulnerability and softness, her lips open the slightest bit, so he could hear her slow breathing, watch her body rise and fall with each breath.

It stirred something inside. A strong protective feeling, of knowing he wanted to wake up with this woman each and every day, be the one next to her when she opened her eyes first thing in the morning, and last thing before she fell asleep at night.

The room, he realized, was frigid again, and carefully he eased away from Quinn to creep over to the fireplace where he pushed around the embers and added more paper and logs, until, satisfied it had taken light, he scampered back to join her.

As if sensing that he—and the heat he brought with him—had returned, she turned toward him, squirming closer. A moment later, her eyelashes fluttered, and she slowly opened her eyes, trying to focus. James had a moment of anxiety wondering what her reaction would be when she realized that everything they'd done last night wasn't a dream but was all too real. That it had really happened.

Her lips curled up into a smile. She looked happy.

"Morning," he said and leaned down to kiss her lips in relief.

"Morning," she said when he broke away and stretched her arms over her head. She shivered immediately as her arms reached the cold air.

"I just put more wood on the fire. Give it a few more minutes," he said, pulling the blanket up and around her, almost tucking her in against the cold. She slid her leg up to rest over his, bringing her body even closer to him. The small action filled him with unexpected satisfaction. "I want to wake up like this every day, you know. With you, naked, in my arms. That's not going to be a problem is it?"

"Not for me. Now, I'm not so sure how my dad is going to take it if he walked in and— Oh. What time is it?"

He looked over at the clock on the microwave. "Almost seven."

She sat up, bringing the blanket with her. "I probably

should get going if I'm going to at least pretend that I slept in my room."

Seeing her go was the last thing he wanted, but he understood the need for some discretion. They had all the time in the world to spend weekends lounging naked in bed together. And as much as he'd joked about her dad meeting him with a rifle, he didn't know how Bill Taylor would take the news of this recent development.

With the blanket still around her, she rose and grabbed her clothes and dashed across the cold floor for the bathroom. A few minutes later, she was back, dressed in some sweat pants and a long-sleeved tee. She eyed her heels that were still abandoned on the floor before heading over to Sabrina's bed where she snagged some slippers. "I'll be back before you know it. Maybe you can get some coffee brewing for us?"

He sat up, grabbing her hand. "So bossy." He kissed her again, enjoying how easy it was, how natural it was to do so. He sighed. "Go before I have you naked and under me again."

She grinned and, grabbing her purse and keys, slipped outside, heading to face whatever might await her.

James grabbed a blanket and headed to the bathroom to quickly shower off before throwing his pants and shirt on and heading over to make a pot of coffee. He'd just flicked on the brew button when the buzzing of his phone on the floor caught his attention. He went over and grabbed it, reading the caller ID.

Immediately, a shadow fell over his mood.

He'd been so wrapped up in this weekend and finding out exactly what his feelings were toward Quinn that he'd nearly forgotten the mess brewing back home. A call from his grandfather sent a sense of foreboding through him, but he answered it, ready to get it over with.

"James." Just a single word was all Cyrus said but it sounded ominous.

"Yes, sir. Is there something wrong?" A reasonable question seeing as how something usually was wrong on those few occasions his grandfather called him directly.

"I could ask the same thing of you. Fortunately, as I'm still on the board of directors, the news was bound to reach me. Anything you'd like to mention?"

The old man knew that the bank was getting nervous, but he apparently wanted to hear James say it. "Well, first off, you might be happy to know that we are in the final stages with the Blossom Brew deal. The bank has some last minute questions to get settled but the approval is as good as ours. And combined with the twenty percent that Thornhill Management will be putting up, everything should be finalized by next week, with a press release by Friday at the latest."

"Is that right? Are you sure about all that? And what about the fact that, without notifying the board, you've gone and fired Thornhill Management's acting general counsel?"

James didn't feel the least bit of remorse in that decision, even now, and it emboldened him as he continued. "It would have been preferable to have had Dennis's replacement already selected and prepared to step in, but sometimes a person is just too poisonous to keep around, and for the good of the company, in the capacity of the acting CEO, I made the call to let him go."

There was a long pause, but James refused to say more, least of all apologize.

"I'm not saying that your reasoning isn't sound, son," Cyrus finally said, his tone almost resigned. "However, as you should know by now, in business, there's always a bit of a game to play. If you wanted Dennis out, there were other ways of going about it. And first and foremost, never make an enemy when you're out of town and out of touch—and completely vulnerable to any accusations he might swing your way to help discredit you to the board."

Discredit him?

"What has he done?" James asked, his tone deadly calm.

"Answer this for me. Where are you exactly? Because last I heard, you were taking a holiday to Mexico with your friends."

"I was, but things got more complicated and I'm in Idaho while they work on the plane."

"This isn't looking good for you. Dennis has been questioning your judgment, particularly when it comes to a certain young lady who I'm gathering you're there with."

Quinn? How did Dennis know anything about her? About them?

As if anticipating James's questions, his grandfather continued. "He's hinted that your decisions are clouded when it comes to this gal. First it started with that employee-assistance plan she wanted, one that several members of the board still have reservations over, and now you're letting her influence you in letting go of a valuable employee with many years of service to this company. Basically, Dennis claims she wanted his job and has used you to that end."

The whole thing was preposterous, but James was careful to keep his anger in check. "Quinn had nothing to do with my decision to fire Dennis. In fact, I haven't even told her. As to the other accusation, my private life isn't Dennis's—or the board's—concern. Dennis is angry, his ego has been damaged, and he wants to stir up trouble. But in time, once the Blossom Brew deal is a go and we get a new general counsel in place, everyone will be back on board."

"You're not really hearing me, son. The twenty percent of the franchise purchase that you need the board to approve is on the line. While you've been away, Dennis has nurtured the doubt of a few on the board, those who've questioned all the changes you want to bring in, and all the costs associated with them. Last I heard, he was close to having the votes he needed to have the board reverse its decision on financing the Blossom deal. And without that twenty percent, you don't have the money to finalize anything. So your ace, this deal, is probably not going to save your ass."

James fumed, not just at Dennis, but over his own shortsighted decision not to fire the guy on the first day he took over, when he had his first qualms about Dennis's loyalty. And now the son of a bitch was going to pound the final nail in his coffin. "How much time do I have until the board votes?"

"They're meeting first thing Wednesday."

In four days.

"Thanks for giving me the heads-up, sir. I'll take care of this."

"James. There's one more thing we need to discuss. About this woman, this Quinn. I don't know what's going on between you two and frankly I don't care. What I need from you is to squash this thing right now. The last thing we need is the two of you showing up looking all gooey-eyed at each other. It would only fuel the fire that Dennis has started and give his theories more credibility."

James felt like the air had been kicked out of him. Give up Quinn? Not a chance in hell.

"I don't care what those old farts think about me and Quinn. I know that nothing has been going on between us up until this weekend, just as I know that Quinn's intentions are honorable. That's what matters."

"You know, I had my doubts when you came back. Doubts that you could keep your eye on the ball and not get distracted. And here you are, almost in the final stretch of putting together something to be proud of, and you're letting your attraction, your—whatever it is you think you're feeling for this woman—get in the way. I might have known you couldn't follow through." Suddenly sounding weary, his grandfather sighed. "Fine, James. You do what you want, as you always do, but don't be surprised when every last member of that board turns away from you and everything you've been working for, giving them the reason they need to kick you out."

The line went dead and James stood there, trying to process what had happened.

How with just a few sharp words, his grandfather could still wound him. Still make him feel like he was sixteen years old and he'd been caught making out in the clubhouse with the twenty-year old daughter of his grandfather's golf buddy. The disappointment in his grandfather's voice that day was much the same as it was just now. Sad, resigned, but not all that surprised.

James wasn't going to disappoint the old man again. He would show him that he meant what he'd said. He would fix this.

First things first. If he couldn't sway the board to front the twenty percent, did he still have time to find another backer? By Wednesday? The outlook was doubtful. And if Dennis had those members in his pocket, like his grandfather thought, everything James had worked for over the past few months was going to be for nothing. He'd lose the deal, and he'd be out. His dream of one day returning to Thornhill Management and showing his grandfather and everyone else that he was as smart, as ambitious, and as savvy as Cyrus Thornhill might have hoped he would be, would be dashed. Permanently.

Then there was Quinn. The one bright star in all of this who made him believe everything was possible. How could he ever give her up?

It was ridiculous. He was a grown man and nothing that he and Quinn had been doing was illegal or immoral. This —this thing that was building between them, wasn't wrong, and he wasn't giving it up. Wasn't giving her up. There would be another solution, there had to be.

The euphoria he'd been experiencing before he'd taken that call was gone, leaving cold anger in its place.

Damn it. He grabbed the phone, scrolling through the numbers to see who he'd call first to do damage control. His heart sank further as he envisioned the conversation he was going to have with Quinn, no matter what he decided. The disappointment he was going to cause her. But there was just too much at stake.

He could only hope that she'd understand.

17

BEARING a tray of stale doughnuts and a box of Nutri-Grain bars, Quinn knocked on the door at the guesthouse then pushed it open. "I hope you're decent. Because I ran into Sabrina inside and it's only a matter of time before she'll be over here to say good morning."

Despite her warning, there was a little pang of disappointment to find James fully dressed and seated on the couch, a couple feet from their makeshift bed, his cell phone to his ear. He waved to her briefly but continued with the conversation.

She studied him from her place at the door. If he didn't shave soon, he was going to actually *be* mistaken for the Brawny guy. But it looked good on him. Really, really good.

Pulling her gaze away, Quinn headed to the counter, where a full pot of coffee was waiting. She poured them both a cup and joined him on the couch while he finished his call.

"All right. We'll talk on Monday. Thank you for making yourself available to me this morning."

"What was that about?"

He took the coffee, his face too grave for this early in the morning. "It's a long story. Not all good."

Whatever it was, it couldn't be that bad. Not when everything was coming together for them.

But five minutes in, after he'd caught her up with his emails and calls with the bank, followed by his decision to fire Dennis, her optimism was waning. "I wish you'd told me about it," she said. Even if he had thought he was doing her a favor by letting her enjoy her vacation unhindered by work problems, she wanted to know these kinds of things because they were important to the company. Important to him.

"It gets worse," he said, eying her warily. "Cyrus called me this morning. It appears that while I've been out of town, Dennis has been undermining me, my authority, everything that I've been working for these past few months. He's created enough unrest that the board is having an emergency meeting on Wednesday to decide whether to reverse their previous decision to use company assets to front the twenty percent on the Blossom deal. Without that money, we won't have enough. And with the short time frame, there isn't time to find someone else to finance that much money. Which means the whole thing might be dead in the water."

No wonder he looked so ripped up. This deal meant so much to him. He'd invested so much time to have it get this far and be at risk of losing it because of some egotistical rat like Dennis. "That's ridiculous. That's like—like cutting off your nose to spite your face. Don't they realize how profitable this deal could be? I don't get it. You had their approval before, which is how things got this far. Why are they second-guessing you now? What could he have said to have changed their opinion?"

He appeared almost pained as he stared at her. "Because

Dennis has put it into their heads that I'm not making decisions right now from a place of power but more a place of... lust. He's insinuated that I've been relying too much on you and your opinions, despite the possible harm it might bring the company. Starting with the EAP and now the decision to let him go. He's saying you wanted his job all along."

A wave of horror and mortification hit her. So many things to process, so many lies. And about her? She almost didn't know where to start. "Dennis is implying that we've been in some sort of sexual relationship from the start? That I've been sleeping with you, seducing you, to get a job I would never want in a million years?"

Quinn felt sick. This was the very reason she'd been reluctant to move their relationship from professional to anything more. Not wanting the knowing looks, the crude jokes, and the credibility she'd worked so hard for lost, just like that.

And the thing that was unfair, up until twelve hours ago —okay, maybe twenty-four if you counted that kiss—she hadn't done anything to cross that line. She could have marched right into that boardroom and denied everything, all the lies that Dennis was spreading to hurt her, to hurt James.

But now...it was true. They were sleeping together, and whether they put a prettier ribbon on it and called it a serious relationship or not, who would believe them?

She leaned forward, covering her hands with her face. This was a mess. How was she going to show her face on Monday? Would there be snickering? Knowing smiles behind her back? Another truth was also starting to hit her. If this deal didn't go through, how long would it be before they were voting to throw James out?

James wouldn't let that happen. She knew that. But what

steps would he take to ensure that didn't happen? What would he need to do to appease the board members who held his future in their hands?

"Don't worry about Dennis's sick innuendo, Quinn. I'll put an end to any conjecture on what our relationship has been. Anyone who knows you would know that you aren't capable of what Dennis is saying. Most of what the board is worried about is the bottom line. And Dennis is making them question that." He sighed, rubbing his beard again absent-mindedly. "It's going to come down to a sacrifice. They'll approve one thing, one risk, but they're not going to approve two. Not right now."

"What are you saying?" she asked, still not getting it.

"It's the cash for the Blossom deal, or the EAP."

Those couldn't be the only solutions. She'd proven in her presentation that the upfront costs were minimal, and the amount of money they could save in the long run would more than make up for that cost. It was why she'd agreed to come on board.

Maybe she could prevail on James to remember why it was so important.

"But—but this plan could help so many employees, employees like my former client, Laurie, like my mother, and countless more who needed earlier access to mental health care. This plan could actually save not just people's jobs, but their lives."

"I know it could. And it will, just..."

From the way that James was looking at her, she was fairly certain which way he was leaning. She tried to tell herself to be rational about it. This decision, letting the EAP fall by the wayside, was probably the worse of two evils. Keeping a deal that would bring actual money to the company, opportunities to its employees, jobs for new employees, verses investing in another insurance plan that would only help employees—at least in the board's eyes—*in theory*.

But she wasn't ready to give up. Not just yet.

"James, I know there's another choice here. There has to be. You're a smart and savvy businessman. You're exactly what this company needs, and you need to make them realize that having you at the helm is in their best interest. You need them to see that they can trust in your decisions."

He sighed. "It's not that easy. Since I walked back in those doors at Thornhill, every decision I've made has been under scrutiny. There were a number of people who didn't think much of me and who were certain that I was going to fail like I've done so often in the past, and then I'd walk away, leaving others to deal with the aftermath. Right now they're waiting for me to fail. To make the wrong call so they can congratulate themselves on something they knew all along. James Thornhill is a screw up."

"I'm sure that's not true, James."

"Right now, I have the opportunity to show them I'm not that screw up. That I can do something right. And this Blossom deal will be the way I can prove that. But Quinn, once this is done, and we're rolling out the stores and bringing in the extra profits, then I'll be in a better position to ask—no, demand, an EAP for our employees. It will be a year, maybe two, tops."

She stared at him, forcing him to meet her gaze again, which he did. "But what about the promise you made me? When you first hired me, you gave me your word that this would be part of the deal of my coming on board."

He flinched. "I know I promised you and I feel horrible about this."

She took in a deep breath, concentrating on slowly

exhaling, letting the air out of her body along with her stress. Trust. She needed to trust him. Even though something she believed so strongly in, knew could be important to so many, was being sacrificed.

But she could be a grown up. She could see that for the greater good that this was the right call.

"There's one more thing, though." This time he grabbed her hand, staring imploringly into her eyes. "This rumor that Dennis is stirring up, about us, it's going to gain a lot of ground before it disappears. And I think, just for a little time, we should hold off on making anything public."

"Of course," she said slowly. "I have as much to lose as anyone. We already agreed that we'd take it slow, keep our relationship outside of work."

"Yes, but"—he paused to scratch the back of his neck —"I think that we need to, at least temporarily, put the brakes on us. Our world is smaller than we think, and it only takes one person to see us out in a romantic capacity to give Dennis's theory credibility."

"You—you want to break up." She swallowed, aware of the lump in her throat, the swelling of pain in her chest.

"No. I don't want to break up. Not at all. But I do think that for a few weeks, maybe even a couple of months, we should slow this down."

It made sense. It was a rational decision. But why did it hurt so much? Why did it feel like the final betrayal? As if her world was spinning out of control?

Just as it had from the first moment she'd thought of James as anything but her boss.

She'd done this. She'd thought that she could relax and maybe see where things might go. And now where was she?

Waiting. Waiting for James to decide when to bring up the EAP again to the board. Waiting for James to decide that it was okay to see her again. Waiting until he decided they could stop sneaking around and make things public. None of which was going to work for her.

No, as she saw it, it was best to put things firmly back in her control, where she at least knew where she stood and she didn't have to risk being hurt.

"Quinn, look—" James started.

But she shook her head forcefully, not needing to hear any more excuses, any more reasons not to do the right thing. Any more reasons to break her heart.

"I have a better idea. Seeing as how we don't want to give anyone the wrong idea about us, I think it would be best that I tender my resignation immediately."

To hell with paying off her student loans, to hell with seeing the zero balance on her mom's medical bills as early as this summer. There was no way she could face this man every day at work and not be reminded of how she feels right now.

Betrayed. Disappointed. Heartbroken.

"You're—you're quitting?" James asked, looking confused at first, and then angry. "I don't understand. Why would you want to do that? We need you at Thornhill. I need you," he said almost desperately. "I know that it's not ideal, us having to take a pause on our relationship, but it's not going to be forever. I'm not planning on seeing any other woman if that's what you're afraid of. You're all I want, Quinn Taylor. I just need to focus right now on getting this done. And then it will be you and me."

"If I was all you wanted, then we wouldn't be where we are right now, James. You'd say to hell with what the board thinks, what your grandfather thinks, and you'd fight for us as much as you're fighting for this deal."

"You're making it sound easier than it is," he said

harshly. "We can have everything we want. It's just going to take time and patience."

She stood, needing to get away from him, distance herself as much as she could. "You know, I think that maybe you should go. Sabrina can drive you into town where you can wait for your car to return you to your plane. You still can take that trip to Cabo, or even get back to the city and work out whatever you have to with the board. I could really use these last couple of days to myself."

He looked torn, and after a moment, he nodded. "You're right. I think we both need a couple of days to think about our priorities. As for your resignation, I'm not ready to accept it. Take some time and you'll see. This can work out."

He took a deep breath, and they studied each other for a long moment. Then, picking up his jacket off the floor, he headed out the door.

While Quinn tried not to feel like her heart was breaking. Again. That someone else she'd begun to care for, maybe even love, hadn't just betrayed her.

QUINN HEARD the door open and the pattering of feet before the mattress dipped as someone sat on the corner of her bed. "Go away," she said, pulling the covers tighter around her head.

"You've been in here all day," Tessa said. "Ever since your flight came in last night. Don't you think you should at least talk to us? Tell us what happened?"

After James had left Idaho yesterday morning, Quinn couldn't bear the questions that would inevitably come from her family and, needing time to herself, had booked the first flight she could find to get back to the city, getting in near midnight last night.

And even though she'd been surrounded by people on the plane and in the airports waiting to depart, she'd felt alone. No one had minded the tear-faced woman in the corner with the earbuds keeping her company.

There was the delicious cracking sound of someone opening a can of soda. "I've got a Coke Zero here if you at least come out of the blanket," Anna cajoled.

What she wouldn't do for that first, bubbly taste... She sat up, throwing the blanket off her.

"Whew—" Anna said, handing her the can. "You might want to consider a shower while you're up." But she was smiling.

The cold beverage tasted good. Even though it only seemed to make her stomach rumble more from hunger.

"I think you'll feel better if you at least talk to us about it. We ordered an extra sausage and pepperoni pizza, your favorite," Tessa added. "It'll be here in ten minutes. Just enough time for you to drag yourself out of bed and take that shower."

Quinn had felt so hollow and sad for the past couple of days. Maybe finally talking about it would help. "Okay."

Fifteen minutes later, the hot water and soap had gone a long way in making her feel almost human again, and she sat on the couch and relayed everything to her best friends. Particularly the part where, after she'd shared the most intimate, amazing night of her life, he'd betrayed her trust by concluding the only way to save his project—his skin—was to sell the project and Quinn out.

The girls surrounded her, hugging her tightly, which, although comforting, brought renewed tears to her eyes.

"We're sorry," Tessa offered.

"Do you want me to write up a blistering piece in an editorial—anonymous, of course—about what a sack of shit they all are?" Anna asked.

That earned a bleak laugh. "No. That's okay. I don't want to hurt the company." Or James.

Her phone vibrated from the coffee table, where it sat next to her drink. They all peered down to see an incoming call from James. That made easily eight. Today.

"What are you going to do?" Tessa asked, almost cautiously. "Are you really willing to give up your job?"

She pushed her hand through her hair. "I don't know, but I can't go back to work like this past week had never happened. Seeing him smile at me and not feel the stabbing pain of betrayal that everything I was supposed to mean to him was a lie."

"If you quit, then you'll no longer have to worry about the rumors," Anna said cautiously. "Do you think you and James might have a chance? That you could find a way to make it work?"

"That's over," Quinn said definitively. "It was over the moment he made our relationship his last priority."

She couldn't come back from that. Ever.

18

JAMES HAD BEEN CERTAIN THAT, after having a couple of days to cool off, Quinn would see reason. That she would see that this was only a temporary delay in their relationship and in the EAP. Something that he had hoped to reiterate when he called her multiple times over the weekend only to find himself in voice mail Siberia.

Somewhere in the back of his head, a voice was telling him that it was over. That Quinn had meant what she said when she'd quit. But he refused to believe it was true, instead hoping that when he arrived to work on Monday morning, Quinn would be in her office defusing any situations that had arisen while she was gone, maybe already scheduling another training session for the next group of managers.

Only Quinn was waiting in *his* office bright and early. Her face tired and drawn and all too vulnerable and his optimism turned to unease.

"You're here. Good," he said, and walked toward her. "I've been trying to reach you for days. I've been worried about you."

She flinched when he sat down next to her and noticeably held her body far from his. A slow-burning panic was starting to set in. This wasn't good.

"I've had some things I needed to work out," she said vaguely.

"I was getting some things worked out as well and I have some good news. I've been in contact with several board members and the doomsday gloom my grandfather pictured isn't quite as bleak as I'd thought. The Blossom deal is not dead and there's still a chance."

"Great. Congratulations." Despite her words, her tone was neutral, robotic even. James studied her, noticing the tired, dark circles under her eyes, eyes that were staring dully back at him. "And the EAP?"

"Quinn. Come on. You know that I don't have a lot of wiggle room here. It was only after I mentioned the possibility of holding off on the program that some of them even started listening to me. As it is, by my last count, I have the votes to pull this off. Barely. It would be foolish for me to try and rock the boat any more than I have by pushing both propositions on them."

"So the EAP is off the table."

"Just for a few months. Until we can show how solvent this new franchise is, and that the small change we lose getting the program up, won't be noticed financially."

"But we already proved that last month, when we were close to having the votes we needed but you pushed it off, until this deal closed."

"I'm asking the board to accept a lot of changes on blind faith in me, a guy many of them wrote off as a slacker long ago. Thanks to Dennis's latest power play, things are rocky. And now that he's gone, I need some time to smooth the waters. But I have some good news," he said, hoping his excitement would be infectious since the cool distance he could sense between them was killing him. "Despite Dennis's attempt to undermine you and everything you've done for the company, most of the members are still supportive of your role here. So although I still think that my grandfather is right and now is not the time to flaunt our relationship, I don't think that we need to wait as long as I originally thought before we can resume things again."

"You don't have to worry about that anymore, or whether the board approves of my role here, because I'm removing myself from the equation. On all fronts." Without meeting his gaze, Quinn handed him a letter he hadn't noticed before.

A growing dread crept over him and he held the letter like it was poison, unable to read the contents. "Tell me what you mean by that. Removing yourself from the equation."

"Just what it sounds like. You're holding my resignation. Ordinarily I'd try and grant you two weeks' notice so you might have time to find a replacement, but under the circumstances, I think it's best that it's effective immediately. It's going to be easier for me if I make a complete break from everything."

"Clean break. You mean from me."

She nodded.

"That's it then?" His voice was louder, sharper than he intended. "Everything we've come to mean to each other these past few months, these past few days, you're going to give it all up?"

"I'm not the one who made the choices here, James. You did that all on your own. Instead of believing in yourself and everything you've been telling me about how you want to make so many changes, positive changes to the company and its employees, you caved the moment it got tough. You are so worried about being the screw-up that everyone thought you were that you stopped fighting for everything that you wanted. Including me."

"I haven't stopped fighting, for you or anything else," he said, his anger shooting up. "Taking a step back, recognizing that sometimes life is about compromise and finding the right moment, is not giving up."

"But you shouldn't have to compromise your ideals to fit into anyone's picture of who you should be," she said sadly. "Don't you think that standing strong, not caving in on issues you believe in, is what makes you not just a better businessman but a better person?"

He came to his feet, his anger needing a way to work itself out as he paced. "Can't you see that I'm trying to keep this company relevant? Profitable? There are tough decisions that have to be made, things that have to be sacrificed along the way, but a strong leader knows this. Knows when to make those calls." His anger left him, leaving him only with the suffocating feeling he was losing her. "I'm sorry that I'm disappointing you. I'm just trying to do the right thing. But I still care about you. I still want to have you in my life. All I'm asking from you is your patience for a little longer."

He reached out to try and take her hand in his, but she pulled it away, shaking her head. "You asked me to trust you once, trust in the possibility of what we could be even though it went against my better judgment. And for a person who usually has to have some semblance of control over her life, that was asking a lot for me, more than I thought I was capable of. But in the end I did trust you and I let go of that control to see where things could go, let myself feel things for someone I knew I had no right to despite the risk. And it was wonderful for as long as it lasted. Until I walked into that room that morning and found the ground falling out from under me. I lost not only a program that I whole-heartedly believe can make a difference in people's lives, but I lost someone who believes he can compromise his ideals and his own heart for the sake of the bottom line. So I lost. And I lost big. Something I won't ever allow myself to do again." She laughed suddenly, but there was no humor in it. "Funny, but that sounds like something I said back in high school after losing a couple of other people who were important to me. You'd think I would have learned."

"You aren't seriously comparing me to them, are you? I haven't betrayed you. I would never betray you. And who the hell are you to sit there and judge me? You have no idea what it's like to be pegged through most of his adult life as a loser, as someone who, given enough time, will manage to screw things up, to fail monumentally. You haven't had the mistakes in your life thrown back at you because you've always been the perfect daughter, perfect friend, perfect student who never knows what it's like to fail. It must be nice to live in a world where people have blind faith that you will do the right thing. Unfortunately, not all of us are similarly blessed. I'm sorry that I am not the perfect man, the man that can meet all your expectations and be the hero you want. This is as good as I get."

"I guess we're at an impasse," she said, rising to her feet. Her chin lifted as she stared at him, her own anger now flashing in her eyes at his words. "I'll reach out to Jeannie and let her know where she can send my things." There was a tightening in his chest now as he watched her walk to the door, and for a moment, there was a shard of hope when she turned around for one last good-bye. "I wish you luck,

James. And I hope this deal is everything you thought it would be—no matter what you lost to get it."

He wanted to bark something back, something that would make her feel a tiny bit of the pain she was causing him right now, but he stopped himself. Instead, he watched the one person he'd thought would always be there for him, understand him, walk out the door.

Back at his desk, he sank into his seat, trying to tell himself he was going to be better off, they were both going to be better off, going their separate ways. They clearly were more different than he'd thought.

If she couldn't understand the responsibilities that came with being a Thornhill, they had no future.

In fact, he should be grateful they figured this out now, rather than before things got more complicated. Before he could get so attached that losing her would be the same heart-ache that he'd experienced when he lost his parent's more than twenty years before.

It had been a close call.

But he was almost certain that he'd caught himself just in time.

"MR. THORNTON, it's nearly ten o'clock," Pauline said from his door on Wednesday morning.

"Thank you," he told his assistant, who was staring at him with mild concern before returning to her desk.

As a precaution, he'd asked Pauline to remind him of the time, not wanting to be late for the board meeting that was going to decide the course for the company in the foreseeable future, even though he hadn't thought it would ultimately be necessary. But the truth was, James had been so lost in his thoughts that he had lost track of the time.

In fact, it felt like he'd lost track of everything that he thought was important to him.

At least James had the confidence that today's vote would go off without a hitch. Having spent the past few days speaking to almost the entire board, he knew he had more than enough votes to affirm the decision to put up the twenty percent financing necessary to complete the Blossom deal. Today's meeting was more a matter of semantics.

And after it was over, he would take the pats on the head from his grandfather and the rest of the board and return to his office knowing that, for someone who had attained everything he thought he wanted, he'd still lost something important, and not just his own integrity. He'd lost something—no, someone—more important.

Quinn.

Even thinking her name brought that suffocating feeling in his chest. In the couple of days since she quit, James had run through all the emotions capable of man. Anger. Frustration. Guilt. Then a deep and sorrowful pain as it really sunk in that Quinn was gone. And the void in his life was more painful than he thought he could bear. Not because she wasn't there to answer the dozens of daily calls and visits from employees and managers who had come to rely on her for expert advice. No it was more than that.

James simply...missed her. He missed her face. He missed her snort when she rolled her eyes at something annoying he'd said. The way she knew the worst things about him but seemed to accept him. He missed the way she'd hid behind those hideous owlish glasses that he would give anything to see right now. The way she would smile at his bad jokes despite herself. He missed how, when they'd made love, she'd given herself entirely to him.

A couple of days ago, he'd told himself it had been good to end things before he was too far deep, too far gone. But now he wondered if that hadn't been a lie since he felt like he'd lost the most important thing in his world.

There was another knock on the door and James looked up expecting to see Pauline with a more dire warning about the time. He hadn't expected to see Cyrus Thornhill standing there.

His grandfather hadn't been into the office since his heart attack. And even though he was still on the board, James hadn't expected he'd be there today for the vote.

He stood. "I didn't expect you today," James said, gesturing to a chair for Cyrus to take a seat.

"I thought it was past time that I came in and saw what you've done for yourself. To mark this important moment for Thornhill Management," he said, coming into the office, but moving toward the window instead of taking a seat. "Pauline tells me you're pretty optimistic that you're going to get the votes you need today."

Good old Pauline—No. He could almost see Quinn rolling her eyes at the term "old" and he nearly smiled. Make that good, reliable Pauline. "Something tells me that you and Pauline must stay in closer touch than I thought."

"I've known her for almost forty years. Of course she's going to keep me in the loop when she can. And lately, she has had some concern over you. Seems to think that you're struggling with something."

"No more than usual." James really didn't want to go into this with the old man. "But if we're going to make it in time to the meeting, we probably should head out."

"They can wait for a minute. How's the hunt going for Dennis's replacement?"

"Better than I thought. I have eight highly qualified applicants I'm interviewing next week. Shouldn't be a problem getting someone in here in no time. In the meantime, our outside law firm is helping us work on anything that can't wait."

Cyrus nodded. "Sounds like you have it well under control. And the other replacement? Pauline mentioned that your employment lawyer—Quinn was it?—also left."

"That replacement is going to be on hold for the time being. No immediate rush."

"It sounds like you made the sound choice there."

"Excuse me?" James asked, trying to keep his temper in check.

"Letting the gal go like that. You knew your responsibilities to the company and you didn't let any other distractions keep you from doing what's right."

James took a moment to get control of his emotions. Because the last thing he would characterize what he'd done in the past few days was the right thing.

It had been the safe thing. The easy thing. But the right thing?

Giving up the one thing he'd promised to Quinn, the one thing that meant so much to her? Something that even he had come to rally behind, seeing it as an example of the changes he wanted to make to ensure the happiness and health of all the employees, that would help him successfully grow this business. That didn't feel right. He'd buckled, like she said, under pressure.

And worse of all, he'd buckled when it came to her. He'd let his fear of losing something that he *thought* was so important to him, lead him to lose the *only* thing of importance. The woman he loved. Just when she had opened herself up to him, let herself believe they could really have a future, he'd pulled back.

Why? Because he'd been stupid and afraid, afraid to stand up for what he knew was right.

Quinn has said something. About standing strong, not caving in on the issues that you believe in. That was what made a real leader. And he could finally see that.

What kind of leader was he if he sacrificed his principles and ideals? If the board couldn't accept this, his grandfather couldn't accept this, then he wasn't the right man for the position, and this wasn't the right place for him to be.

He'd been working from a place of fear, fear of letting people down for so long, and he was done with it.

James leveled his gaze at his grandfather who had been studying him quietly all this time, a curious expression on his face. "I was wrong. I was wrong to let my fear of losing this deal let me lose sight of some more important things. Like honoring a promise to a woman I love. Worst, letting the woman I love think that anything else was more important than her."

"Really? You're willing to give up everything you've been working so hard for, just to prove to this woman that you love her?"

"I sure as hell am," James said with certainty. "And I'm going to go back before that board and tell them why we need to approve that EAP now, not in the future, not months down the road, but today and merely because it's the right thing to do. I'm going to let them know that over the past few months, I've fallen in love with a brilliant and caring and generous woman who happened to be an employee of this company, and if they don't like it, then they can look for another man for the job. I'm sorry if that disappoints you. I know that you didn't choose me for this job and that you've had to watch from afar, worried I'd mess this up. But I have done my best here and you're going to have to be satisfied with that."

James stared at his grandfather, surprised that he'd finally had the strength to say exactly how he felt, and how good it felt to be so honest, no matter the old man's reactions.

Even if, from the slow smile spreading on his face, Cyrus looked far from angry or disappointed.

"Did you really think that it was the board who had chosen you, sought you out to just temporarily take on this role?" He shook his head. "No, I've been waiting for the day that you were ready to come back here, hoping you'd come in on your own. When I had my heart attack, even through the pain and terror of not knowing what was happening to me, I was certain of one thing. That you were the man for the role and I said as much. No one was surprised either, as most of them knew you and knew what you were capable of. I know you've made mistakes in the past, who hasn't. But I knew you'd grow from them and become a better man. As you have. If you think that this employment program is a good idea, then that's good enough for me. It you believe that you're in love with this woman, and she's as wonderful as you think she is, that's also good enough for me."

James couldn't believe what he was hearing. The warm affection in his grandfather's eyes. His belief that James was the first and only choice to head Thornhill Management.

He cleared his throat, overwhelmed with the emotions that his grandfather's speech had aroused. "I had no idea you felt that way," he said, his voice just above a whisper.

"Yes, well, it's first for both of us. This honesty. You remember my nurse, Jenny? Well, she's made me take some accounting of my life as of late. Made me see what I've been missing and I'd hate for you to do the same."

James remembered the nurse, of course. She'd been one of the few people that Cyrus actually listened to in the few times James had observed them together. He hadn't thought anything of it then, but now, he was looking at things in a new light. The indulgent smile she had given Cyrus, not putting up with the old man's cantankerous and bossy ways, not to mention his grandfather's own begrudging acceptance at doing his exercises, or of giving up the alcohol and treats he usually enjoyed, all because Jenny had said so.

"Are you two together?"

"We're figuring things out. But that's not what we're here to discuss today. Have you told this woman how you feel?"

James smiled. He wasn't going to be afraid. He believed in his vision; he believed in himself and his capabilities. And he believed in his love for Quinn.

Just as she had wanted for him all along.

"She'll know soon enough. First, I have a few things I need to get settled with the board."

19

JAMES NEARLY SKIPPED up the stairs leading to Quinn's place. His relief and excitement that the board had agreed to sign off on the financing *and* the EAP was nothing to his relief and excitement at finally telling Quinn everything she'd come to mean to him.

That he loved her, and he hoped she could forgive him for being too blind and stupid and afraid to see that before.

He rang the doorbell and waited, his heart racing as he wondered what she would say when she saw him, if she'd even open the door to let him explain. He'd tried calling her again, of course, but that call, like the others, had gone straight to voice mail.

He leaned in, trying to hear if anyone was possibly on the other side of the door, watching him and deciding to let him in. Maybe she wasn't even home. That thought nearly deflated him, as the urge to see her right now was overwhelming.

He pounded on the door.

"Coming," someone called out. It wasn't Quinn, but at

least it was someone who could tell him when she'd be back.

The door swung open and the blonde roommate, the reporter, stared back at him.

"Quinn isn't here," she said with a definite edge in her tone before he could utter a word. She crossed her arms in front of her.

"Anna, is it?" She didn't argue so he assumed he was correct. "Do you know when she'll be back? Or perhaps where I might find her?"

"Why? What more do you have to say that wasn't already said?"

"I need to speak to her. I need to apologize, to tell her I love her and a lot of other things but—don't take this the wrong way—I'd prefer she heard it all from me first."

Anna studied him, her face still drawn in doubt.

"Please?"

She heaved a sigh. "Fine, but Quinn's at an interview at the Parker building downtown and won't be back for at least another hour."

He didn't wait, instead turning around and racing back down the stairs. "Thank you, Anna. I owe you one."

By the time he was in the car and gave his driver directions, Anna was already back inside.

James stared ahead, seeing the Parker building soar before him. She was there, inside, the woman who his entire future was bound to, and who didn't even know it.

He barely waited for the car to stop before he threw the door open, not sure where she was, but determined that he would find her.

❋

"THANKS again for meeting me like this, John," Quinn said, rising to her feet.

"It was my pleasure. To be honest, I couldn't believe my luck when you called me yesterday and to say you were moving back into private practice. We'll be in touch by tomorrow with a proposal."

She smiled and shook his hand. It was almost surreal to be here meeting with one of the top labor and employment law firms in the city that specialized in representing plaintiffs. Particularly considering how far she'd come these past couple of years since leaving her big job at Spencer Hautner in what felt like disgrace because she couldn't hack it.

But this place would be different. It might not pay her as much as she'd made at Thornhill, but she'd be doing exactly what she wanted to do, protecting exactly who she wanted to protect, without treading lightly around the big egos at Thornhill Management.

It would be a good fit. And it would help her put James and his company behind her once and for all.

The elevator was crowded, and she stepped to the back, waiting patiently to reach the first floor. For a moment, as the doors shut, she thought she saw someone who looked a lot like James getting off the elevator across the way. But then again, she'd been seeing James everywhere, eyes open or shut, over the past few days, so it didn't really give her reason to pause.

It was nearly noon, and the sun was pushing through the clouds on a slightly foggy day when she spotted the coffee cart out front. Exactly what she needed. A sentiment that was shared by half a dozen people already in line in front of her.

It took her a minute to notice that someone joined the

line behind her, standing close enough to cast a shadow over her.

"You know, if it's coffee you like, I have the inside track on a hot new franchise deal with a nationally recognized coffee chain."

She wouldn't look at him. She *couldn't* look at him. Instead, she kept her attention on the guy in line in front of her and took a step forward as the line progressed. "I'm just fine, thank you."

Whatever new game James was playing, she wasn't going to bite.

"Our flagship Blossom Brew store should be opening in the next couple of months. Around the same time that the new employee assistance plan rolls out to all our employees."

Had she heard him correctly? The program—her program—was a go? She risked a glance his way, not sure if she liked the way he was smiling at her. "I'm glad to hear that you realized how valuable this program could be for your employees."

She took another step forward in line. If he expected her to jump up and down and throw her arms around his neck as if all was forgiven, he was sorely mistaken.

"That's right. I can see you're restraining yourself from showing your excitement. You were also right, about how I needed to believe in me, about not being afraid. When it came time to speak before the board this morning, I found your words echoing in my head. Well, that and a few other things that made me realize how much I missed you, but I digress. The point is, I didn't compromise. I laid out again why the EAP was a sound business decision, why letting go of Dennis was the best thing for the future of the company, and why they needed to put their full faith in me so I can do my job."

He had? He'd done all that? She wanted to ask him how it'd gone, but she stopped herself. No. Whatever happened at Thornhill Management or happened with James Thornhill no longer concerned her.

Another step forward. The guy in front of her was giving his coffee order.

"You might also be relieved to hear that the board won't be throwing me out any time soon. Not that that would have changed what I'd said. Standing up for what I believed in was the right thing to do, I only wish I'd realized it sooner. Before I lost someone who meant a great deal to me. Before I lost you."

She bit her lip, wanting to throw back at him that she'd wished he'd realized it sooner too. Before it was too late. But she wasn't speaking to him.

"I know that right now you're mad at me, and justifiably so. I was an ass, and after asking you to trust me, I betrayed that trust and hurt you. I'd give anything if I could take that moment back that moment when I saw the pain and disappointment in your eyes. I was afraid to fail and wasn't yet ready to believe I could do it all fully on my own. You believed in me, though, more than anyone has for a long time."

She felt a lump in her throat. The line was totally clear in front of her now. But she was having a hard time moving.

"Are you ordering something or not?" the coffee guy asked in a tone that led her to believe he'd been waiting longer than that moment.

She stepped up, aware of James stepping up along with her. "A small latte, please."

"Five twenty-five."

Oh, right. Money. She fumbled through her handbag until she found her wallet and opened it.

Damn. She'd used the last of her cash for the cab to get here.

From the corner of her eye, she saw someone holding out a twenty-dollar bill.

The coffee-cart guy cleared his throat, and she sensed some frustration from the people behind her, waiting for her to do something.

"Fine. But it's only a loan," she said, taking the money without meeting his eyes. "You can have it deducted from my last check."

"Fair enough."

She handed it over to the coffee guy, who made the change, then started her latte.

"Let's see. Where was I? That's right. I want you to take whatever time you need to process everything, see if you might reach the point where you can forgive me. Because I don't think I've expressed my profound regret at thinking for one second that I couldn't be honest about my feelings for you. To the board, to my grandfather, or even to myself. It took losing you to realize how much you've come to mean to me. How much I love you and miss having you in my life."

She looked up at him in surprise. Had he said...?

"That's right. I love you, Quinn Taylor. And I know—" The sound of the machine frothing the milk cut James off, and he paused for a moment until the whirring stopped before starting again. "I know that I have a lot to prove to you, to show the true depths of my feelings where you're concerned."

That she hadn't expected. And she sucked in a breath,

trying to understand why her heart was hammering again. It had been broken, right? Shattered. Nothing could salvage it.

"Now I know you're probably secretly snorting inside, that you're undoubtedly having a hard time believing it's possible that someone as seemingly selfish as me could love anyone. But it's true," he continued, even though she hadn't given him the least encouragement. "And I promise I will never give you a reason to doubt my word. Because you're the only person I want to see when I close my eyes at night, the first person I want to see when I wake up. You're the person I want to call bullshit when I say something's impossible. Who makes me laugh one minute and then makes me want to kiss you senseless the very next. Who will sit there with your owlish glasses on your cute face appearing as prim and proper as a schoolmarm before pulling on the fishnet tights and roller blades and taking out everyone who gets in your way."

He stopped, and she knew he was waiting for her to look at him, but she was almost afraid to, only making it this far by refusing to stare into those deep blue eyes, eyes that would make it impossible to say no to. But one thing she wasn't was a coward. If this was it, if that's what she intended, she needed to at least face him.

Taking a breath, she raised her eyes to meet his. Just as she'd thought. His eyes were soft, and despite the hope that was in their depths, there was also sadness. "Quinn, you're the one person I want to spend the rest of my life making happy."

Someone cleared their throat. Twice.

Right. Her coffee.

The guy looked relieved when she took it and stepped away.

James hadn't taken his gaze from her. She studied him, trying to figure out what was different. "You—you shaved." Her hand reached out automatically to graze against the smooth surface, but she stopped herself in time. Especially when, now, from this angle, she could see that they'd drawn quite an audience behind them.

"After all I just said to you, that's all you have to say?" He smiled, though, tenderly. Hitting her heart all over again.

"Sorry. I'm still processing." Because for the past few days, Quinn had been telling herself that nothing this man could ever say would make right what had happened. That it was truly over. And she could remember how sure and resolute she'd been at the time.

Only right now, the sadness and despair that had led up to that decision were no longer there. They'd been replaced with something else. Something warm and bright and joyous, something that was giving her a reason to believe in him again.

"Do you mean it?" she asked in almost a whisper.

"Which part? About the roller blades and fishnet stockings?"

She rolled her eyes, knowing the moment she did that she'd done exactly what he'd expected her to. He did know her, sometimes too well. "The part where you said you loved me."

"Ah, that part. Yes, I'm afraid it's true. It's also true that I said some terrible things, things that I didn't mean, and I sincerely hope you can forgive me."

"I—I think I already have." And the minute she said it, she knew it was true, and it felt like the weight of the world had lifted from her shoulders.

He took a step forward, his eyes wide with hope, and she could see him fighting the urge to reach out and touch her, just as she did him. "And are you willing to give me—give us —another try?"

Was this really happening? The guy who she knew she was completely head-over-heels in love with was standing here and telling her he loved her? That he wanted to spend the rest of his life making her happy?

"So what do you say?" he tried again.

She took a deep breath, hoping that she could find the right words. "Maybe you weren't completely wrong about me. About my not knowing what it's like to have the people around me doubt me, to think that my failure is inevitable. I've been lucky. I've always had the love and vocal support of my family and it's something I've probably taken for granted. And contrary to your opinion of me, I'm not perfect." At his look of feigned horror, she laughed. "I do make mistakes and I am going to need you to remind me that I'm not always right. That things aren't always black and white, right or wrong."

He pretended to write something on his hand. "Quinn... makes...mistakes. Got it." He looked up, his lips twisted in that smile of his that had her heart battering against her chest. "Anything else?"

She took the last steps forward so they were almost touching and she gazed up at him, her heart on her sleeve. "Just that, for the record, I knew I loved you almost from the start. And I haven't stopped loving you, no matter how much I tried. You're in my heart. So remember that, remember that I love—"

The rest was cut off as he took that last step forward, his mouth crushing down on hers, and for the first time in a long time, she was able to breathe again. She sighed as she leaned into him, loving the warm comfort of his arm wrapped around her waist. Not even caring about the scene they were creating or the soft applause as people cheered them on.

Because she knew that here, in this man's arms, was exactly where she belonged.

EPILOGUE

"CONGRATULATE ME," Quinn said nearly two months later as she stepped into James's office looking dangerously sexy in a modest knee-length skirt contrasted against black high heels. Not the frumpish, matronly and ever practical heels she wore when they'd first met, but the kind that gave him visions of her wearing the shoes—and nothing else.

He pushed back in his seat, smiling at the flush of excitement that flooded her face. She definitely had his attention.

"Not only did I nail that deposition with the HR manager, but their attorney already reached out to me to talk about settlement."

"Naturally. You're Quinn the Ter-Quinn-a-tor and I wouldn't expect anything less." He went to his door and shut it, affording them a little privacy, before returning to his desk. Taking a perch on the corner, he wrapped his arms around Quinn, holding her close to him for a long-awaited kiss. Something he'd been waiting all day for.

She sighed and leaned her head against him. He couldn't imagine his life being any better.

Initially, after they'd made up, James had been resistant

to the idea of Quinn working anywhere but Thornhill Management. But in the days and weeks since, he'd come to realize that, where she was working, doing what she was doing, helping clients who needed a voice, was the best thing for them both. It certainly made it easier that they didn't have to butt heads when they disagreed over how a personnel matter should be handled. Something told him that had he tried to pull rank on her on any such issue, it wouldn't have gone very well.

Then there was the truth in the saying about absence making the heart grow fonder, because he knew that up until she'd walked in that door, he'd been counting the seconds until he saw her again.

The phone suddenly rang from his desk and Pauline's voice filled the room. "Mr. Thornhill? Your grandfather wanted to remind you that he's meeting with you and the reporter in ten minutes to discuss the Blossom Brew grand opening."

"Thanks, Pauline. Tell him I'll meet them in the conference room."

"Are you sure that our leaving this weekend is a good idea?" Quinn asked him, still in his arms. "There has to be a ton of things that you need to finalize and—"

"There's nothing more important than making it back to your hometown for your dad's birthday. As long as you're sure he's not going to shoot me on sight." James knew that when he spoke briefly on the phone with Quinn's dad, he'd *seemed* to be okay with the idea of James and his daughter being a couple. Especially now that she was back out there again in private practice—and not working for him.

But he probably wouldn't be taking any fishing trips with the man until he was certain.

"Dad and Mom are both happy that *I'm* happy. Believe me."

"And Sabrina is okay with our staying out in the guesthouse, leaving her to bunk in her old room again?"

She ran her hand through his hair, tousling it for a moment, her touch something he was never going to get tired of. "Well, I might have had to offer her a little bribe to get her to come fully to terms with that proposal. But since we have those tickets, it only makes sense that we let her use them."

"Yeah. A weekend in a one-room rustic guesthouse in your parent's backyard is definitely an even trade for a one week getaway in June to romantic Italy at the world's finest luxury hotels," he teased.

She smiled. "It was a thoughtful gesture, though, and if I didn't have that big trial against the city that same month, I would have loved nothing more.

"Another time." He kissed her again, enjoying the feel of her lips under his, knowing exactly how to apply the right pressure.

She sighed and pulled away. "*That* is going to have to wait until after dinner tonight. In fact, you probably should go. I hate to think that you're keeping your grandfather waiting."

That was another thing, who'd have thought that once they got to know each other, that Quinn and his grandfather would have so much in common? In fact, sometimes James felt like the third wheel when they got together, a feeling that was staved off by his grandfather's new girlfriend, Jenny, who still hovered around, making sure Cyrus had everything he needed.

Even after all these years, it was nice to see Cyrus find someone to love.

"I think Cyrus Thornhill will manage just fine without me."

"Probably. But it still doesn't change my mind."

"Fine. You win. I'll go."

She laughed. "You act like I'm sending you to the gallows when it took you three weeks to convince that reporter to come in for the exclusive. You know, the sooner you go, the sooner you're done, and the sooner I can show you the little something I bought the other day. Something I'm pretty sure you're going to like."

"Is that right?" Reluctantly, he pulled away and went to his chair to grab his jacket, taking a moment to button it up. "How do I look?"

The long languid gaze she gave him, her lips turning up in appreciation, nearly undid him. And for a minute, James just stared down at the woman he was irrevocably in love with. Who made everything in the world seem possible, who made him feel like he could do anything as long as they were together.

"You know I love you, right?"

She leaned forward with a grin before kissing him within an inch of his life before pushing him away and to the door. "Of course I do. I knew it long before you did."

He smiled, making sure she heard him as he headed out. "Of course you did."

Yeah. She was definitely going to keep him on his toes, was going to fill his life with unexpected joy.

And love.

WANT TO HEAR ABOUT ANY UPCOMING RELEASES?

Subscribe to my newsletter and stay up to date on the latest releases, cover reveals, and giveaways! Click HERE or type in the link: http://bit.ly/2cd3SvQ

ALSO BY ASHLEE MALLORY

Sweet Contemporary Romance

Crazy in Love Series:

Crazy for the Boss

Crazy for the Best Man

Crazy for the ___ (Coming Soon!)

Sorensen Family Series:

Her Backup Boyfriend

Her Accidental Husband

The Playboy's Proposal

Her Surprise Engagement

Romantic Suspense

You Again

Love You Madly

Thriller

Deceived

ABOUT THE AUTHOR

Ashlee Mallory is a *USA Today* Bestselling author of sweet romantic comedy, suspense, and thrillers. A recovering attorney, she currently resides in Utah with her husband and two kids. She aspires to one day include running, hiking, and traveling to exotic destinations in her list of things she enjoys, but currently settles for enjoying a good book and a glass of wine from the comfort of her couch.

Ashlee loves to hear from readers. You can find her at any of the following links, so please feel free to drop her a line, or subscribe to her email list and keep updated with any news of upcoming releases, sales, and giveaways by clicking here: Newsletter.

You can also find her on:

Facebook | Twitter | ashleemallory.com | Goodreads